The Adventures of
PREACHER PUSS

a novel by
Richard G. Edwards

[signature]

To my Friend and fellow
HHS classmate John
David Martin,
I hope you enjoy my book!

Pax Tecum!   Dick Edwards
                    4/21/18

Front Cover
The author took the photograph of his cat Smoky appearing on the front cover of this book.

Back Cover
The tessellation used as background for the back cover was drawn by the author's wife Carolyn.

Acknowledgements

Dr. Bill Green, Mr. Jack Sterling, Dr. Gus Peters, Mrs. Rita Schrodt, Mrs. Ann Knapp, and my wife Carolyn provided many excellent suggestions, comments, and corrections for this novel. I extend my sincere appreciation to them. The expert layout of the book was accomplished by Mrs. Kelly Elliott, who resides in Naples, Italy. I'm so thankful for the miracle of the internet and grateful for her assistance.

Pax Tecum!

Dedication

This book is dedicated to all cat lovers. Before I was married, over 52 years ago, I was a true dog lover. I never had a cat. That all changed when Carolyn and I were married in 1966. She loved cats. Soon after marriage we adopted our first feline, Thomas. He lived to the ripe old age of 18, and after he passed we acquired many other cats over the years until in 2009 Smoky came along (see below). He was very special!

Smoky Edwards
2009 - 2015

Smoky Edwards was found by our son Kyle as a young stray kitten wondering the campus of Lindsey Wilson College in Columbia, Ky. Kyle brought him (yes, Smoky was a "he") to Lexington and gave him to us in 2009. He quickly became a very loved member of our family. He made the snowbird trips with us each year to Florida. Sadly, on Feb. 23rd of 2015 he was diagnosed with terminal cancer and was euthanized to prevent suffering. It was a very sad day.

**Smoky Edwards
aka Preacher Puss**

But Smoky will live on in the pages of my novels where he was the inspiration for the 15 pound gray tabby cat named "Preacher Puss" who takes up residence in the office of the Harlan County Sheriff and is quickly established as an enforcer of law and order.

Smoky Edwards, gone.....but not forgotten!

Preface

This effort represents my seventh novel. The first five (*Anchor Cross Series*), the sixth (*Nuclear Attack*), and this current book each have many of the same mountain characters, and are all set in Harlan County, Kentucky. I've tried my best to include a lot of mountain stories and humor reflecting my Kentucky heritage, of which I'm very proud. I've received much feedback from those reading my books, and I truly value it. If you have not read my prior novels, I'll list them below. They are all available from Amazon.com and Barnesandnoble.com, or directly from me by just sending a request to my email, as follows:

RICHARDGLENNEDWARDS@GMAIL.COM

I would also greatly value any comments you might care to share with me.

A list of my previous books:

#1   *Anchor Cross Second Edition*
#2   *The Pelle Anchor Cross*
#3   *The Helena Anchor Cross*
#4   *The Anchor Cross Twins*
#5   *The Constantine Anchor Cross*
#6   *Nuclear Attack*

Pax Tecum!

CHAPTER 1
HARLAN, KENTUCKY

I am a cat. My real name is Smoky, but most everyone calls me Preacher Puss. I'll tell you about that a bit later. I reside in the Office of the Harlan County, Kentucky sheriff, J. Bert Sterling. Sheriff Sterling is really a very nice guy, and I like him a lot. But his deputy, Rosie Cain, is my master, and I truly love Rosie. She looks after my every need and is very kind to me. I've got to be about the luckiest cat in the world. And I've even gained quite a reputation as one of Sheriff Sterling's most valuable assets. So I guess I'm a little unusual for a cat, but we'll talk more about that later as well.

Let me tell you how I came to be here in the sheriff's office. My earliest memory is being in an animal shelter in Cumberland, Kentucky, a town about 25 miles Northeast of Harlan on route 119. I was just a young kitten and had no memory of my parents or siblings. One day two very nice men came to the shelter and when they saw me they told the employee there that they wanted to adopt me. I remember they were very gentle, and gave me lots of pets and talked to me saying they were going to take me to their farm. They had brought a cat carrier with them, and I was very frightened when they first put me inside it, but it had a nice blanket on its floor and I cuddled up and slept the entire trip to their farm. I later found out that the two men were brothers, the Slusher brothers. Their 50 acre farm was located off highway 119 about midway between Harlan and Cumberland. The brothers, nicknamed Gunsmoke and Booger, were very wealthy. They were cat lovers, and after I arrived I soon learned that they had about 20 other cats on their farm. I had lots of company, and soon made friends with most of them. When they first got me to their farm home, Booger sat in a chair at one end of their great room and Gunsmoke sat in a chair across the room. Booger sat the cat carrier with me inside down on the floor in front of him and opened the door. I bounded out and started running across the room toward Gunsmoke. I guess I must have looked like a little bundle of grey, smoky fur to Gunsmoke, because as I was running to him he said, "Booger, this kitty's name has got to be Smoky. With that smoky grey hair it seems a fitting name." Booger nodded his head affirmatively and replied, "Smoky she will be!" And that's how I got my name.

After living with the Slusher brothers for about a year, one day I went out exploring the farm. I had done this many times before, but today was a lovely day and it just seemed wonderful to be outside. The farm had a very high fence all around it, so I had never been outside that fence. I walked over to the entrance gate. It was located about a quarter mile from the house. A very nice man whose name was Charlie worked for the Slusher brothers as a guard at the gate. When Charlie saw me he came out of the gate house and walked over to me and said "Good Morning Smoky" and gave me several gentle strokes. He then reached into his pocket and pulled out a "Whisker Lickin" cat treat and offered it to me. Because there were so many cats on the farm, Charlie was always prepared with cat treats and all the cats knew it. He was a popular fellow! I readily accepted the treat, then looked at Charlie with my best wishful expression hoping for another one. But just then a truck pulled up and Charlie began to trot back into the guard house. He opened the window facing the truck and I heard him say, "Hey Ray, did you find what you needed? Ray, who also worked for the Slusher brothers running errands and doing anything that needed to be done, said, "Yep, Charlie, found just what I needed at Wal-Mart. If Wal-Mart ain't got it, you don't need it!". And then Charlie pressed the button that opened the gate to allow Ray to drive through. I guess Charlie forgot about me standing beside the gate. When it swung open I thought I'd take the opportunity to see a little of the world beyond the Slusher farm and ran out the gate. In retrospect, that wasn't such a good idea. Charlie saw me, but by then I was well down the road. He started running after me, but I was determined to explore and easily outran him.

I continued down the road a ways, and then decided to wander off into the woods. After walking for about an hour I came to a dilapidated old house. I was getting a bit thirsty and thought I might get lucky and find some water around the house and as I was exploring two other cats appeared. I didn't know if they lived at the house or not, but they came walking out of the woods some distance from the house. When they saw me we all started the hissing contest at each other, not knowing if friend or foe. After reaching each other, and then doing our usual smelling, it seemed mutually agreeable that we could be friends. So the hissing ceased and our fur relaxed and we just looked at one another, each trying to think what the next move would be. Just then a mean looking man emerged from the back door of the house. He had in his hand what I later learned was called a pistol. He walked slowly toward us cats saying "Here kitty, kitty." We just watched him. When he got about six feet from us he lifted up his hand holding the pistol and fired it. One of the other two cats got hit by what came from the pistol and slumped to the ground. He fired the gun again at the other cat. As he did I sprang away and ran as fast as I could toward the woods. I heard another shot and saw dirt fly up just in front of me. Then another shot and dirt flew beside by head just as I reached the woods, and then the shooting stopped. I turned and looked back. I saw the mean man walk over to the two dead cats and kick them with his foot and say, "No trespassing allowed on my land. And if your buddy comes back he'll join you among the dead." I definitely wasn't going back. And I'll always remember what that pistol did, and anytime in the future that I see one of them I'll do everything I can to prevent it from being used. I continued through the woods.

I had walked for about an hour, and then I saw it! A bear!! I had seen bears before, but only from the safety of being inside the fence at the Slusher farm. I had watched them roam just outside the fence, and always thought how terrible it would be to encounter one without the fence between us. I now had that experience. And it was a big bear. Its fur was black, and it had to weigh many hundred pounds. It was only about 25 feet from me and appeared to be eating something. It was turned to the side and hadn't noticed me. I quickly lowered myself to the ground, and watched the bear. And then the bear lifted his nose into the air and appeared to be sniffing it......and then turned and looked directly toward me. I guess I must have been upwind from him, and he smelled me. Trouble, big time! He then sprang toward me, much faster than I thought something that big could. I jumped straight up, did a 180 degree turn, and ran for my life. I could hear the bear closing in on me. There was a tree directly in my path so I thought I'd climb it to where maybe the bear couldn't reach me. I shot up the tree. It wasn't a large tree, and I made it about as far up as I could. But I was only about 15 feet above the ground. The bear got to the tree and raised up on its hind legs. It wrapped its front legs around the tree trunk and started to climb. It was then that I realized bears could climb trees! Not a good time to find out. The bear slowly moved up the tree until his head was only a few feet below me. I knew I had to do something, or else become the bear's lunch. I shifted a bit, and then, with all claws extended, dropped directly into the face of the bear. All four of my paws landed on his snout and the claws dug in. The bear growled loudly and removed one of his forelegs from around the tree trunk in order to hit me with it. But when he did, he started to fall....with me attached to his snout. Blood was starting to stream down the bear's face, and as he hit the ground I jumped as far as I could away from him and started running for my life. When I didn't hear any noise behind me I dared to glance back. I guess the bear decided he had enough of me and was sitting at the base of the tree wiping the blood from his face. I breathed a big sigh of relief, and continued my journey.

After wandering for the rest of the day I was very tired, hungry, and thirsty. When night arrived I just found a bed of leaves and curled up for the night. The next morning after wandering for a while through the woods I realized that I was lost. I had no idea how to get back to the Slusher farm. What was I going to do? I sure wished I had not elected to run through the open gate and explore. It was indeed a bad mistake. I continued to walk through the woods for several more hours, and finally came to a clearing that was a parking lot for a church. The church itself was located on the main road. I thought surely I can find some water around there and even perhaps some food, so I trotted down into the parking lot. As I was looking for water and food a truck pulled into the parking lot immediately in back of the church. The sign on the truck said "Giles Janitorial Services". A man got out of the truck and walked to the back, opened the doors, and removed some brooms, mops, and buckets. I strolled up beside him and rubbed against his ankles, hoping he would reward me with food or drink. He looked down at me and said, "Get out of here cat. I got work to do." My luck was not running good. He took his load and walked to the rear church door and opened it and went inside. I thought surely that church has water available.....I'll just run in before he sets his load down and closes the door. I slipped in behind him without his knowing. I was then careful to hide behind boxes so he couldn't see me. He then went to a maintenance closet, opened it, and put his bucket under a water faucet and started filling it. The sound of that running water sure was joy to my ears. As he filled his bucket he reached into his pocket and pulled out a cigarette and put it in his mouth. He then reached into another pocket and pulled out a lighter and lit his cigarette. He finished filling the bucket and then added something to it and carried it and his brooms off to another location in the church. I walked in the little closet where he got his water, jumped up on the sink, and saw that there was a good drip coming from the faucet. I started licking it.....ahh, sweet relief! After several minutes of licking my thirst was quenched. I jumped back down on the floor and wandered around looking for the man, and to see if I could locate food. The man was busy mopping in the sanctuary, and I didn't see any food anywhere. Well, at least my thirst was satisfied. I thought I'd just find a good safe place behind a box in the back room and take a little nap, which I did. I slept much longer than intended, and when I woke I smelled smoke. I ran into the sanctuary to see if the man was still there... he was not. And there were flames jumping from the door to the maintenance closet. The man must have left his cigarette in the closet and it somehow caught something on fire. Smoke was really rolling out of the closet, and the flames were getting larger!! How can I get out of here? I was very concerned that I was getting ready to need one of my nine lives!

Just as I ran to the back room hoping that the door might be open I heard a faint siren. And it kept getting louder. It soon was very loud and then someone was beating on the back door. The next thing that happened scared me so much that I jumped straight up in the air. The person trying to get in apparently kicked the door real hard and wood started to splinter and I saw a foot come through the door's wood and saw daylight outside. A hand then reached through the hole made by the foot and reached up and unlocked the door. It flew open and four fireman came rushing in pulling a fire hose. The front fireman opened the nozzle on the hose and water began to spurt out in a very large stream. They headed toward the sanctuary. All the church was filled with dense smoke, and the firemen wore breathing masks. They located the fire and put it out quickly. As they were returning the hose back to their fire truck the pastor of the church showed up and walked inside the back room, but stayed close to the door so he could breathe. A couple of the fireman came to him and they talked. I looked up at them and gave my very loudest and longest "meow". After repeating it quickly several times one of the firemen spotted me. He walked over and gently lifted me up into his arms. He stroked my fur and told me I was going to be okay. He then walked over to the pastor and asked if I was his cat. The pastor said, "No. I don't know how the cat got into the church, but it doesn't belong to anyone I know." I gently meowed. Several times. The fireman then said they would have to get me to a vet to be checked out, and would then take me to the sheriff's office. And that they did.

The vet examined me all over. She put things down my throat and gave me some medicine. I really didn't like it, but I knew she was trying to help me. So I went along with it. She then told the fireman that I would be fine in a couple of days, and that I should continue to take my medicine.....she said it would help clear my lungs. The fireman then took me and the medicine and headed for the office of the Harlan County sheriff in downtown Harlan.

Perhaps I should tell you that I'm a pretty good size cat. I am a grey tabby and then weighed about 15 pounds. When the fireman walked through the door to the sheriff's office he was carrying me in his arms in a blanket. My head, with ears perked up, was looking all around. When he entered the office the deputy behind the desk, Rosie Cain, saw me and said, "Ahhh, isn't that an adorable cat. What in the world are you doing bringing her here to the sheriff's office?"

The fireman explained what had happened, and said that no one claimed the cat, and they didn't know what else to do with her other than to bring her to the sheriff's office. Rosie rushed over to the fireman and took me in her arms and started petting and talking to me. I could immediately tell we were going to be the best of friends. Rosie told the fireman, "Okay, just leave her with me. I'll have to convince Sheriff Sterling that the office needs her for a mascot. It likely won't be easy, but the beautiful yellow eyes and gorgeous long grey hair should be a big help." I purred my approval loudly.

Now we come to the part in my story where I got the name Preacher Puss. After the fireman left and Rosie sat holding me in her lap and petting me, she said to me, "Kitty, we've got to have a name for you." I really wanted to tell her my name was Smoky, but one of the limitations the good Lord gave us cats is that we can't do human talk. I just purred and looked at her. "Well, the fireman said he found you in a church screaming at the top of your lungs. So I think an appropriate name would be Preacher Puss!" I thought about that for a minute, and thought it to be a bit of a strange name, but if it pleased Rosie then henceforth I would answer to Preacher Puss. I gave forth an approving meow.

Just then the door to the sheriff's office opened and a very handsome man walked in. He was all dressed neatly in a uniform. Rosie, still sitting in a chair and holding me, looked up and said, "Hi Bert, lookie what I've got!"

Harlan County Sheriff J. Bert Sterling looked at Rosie, got a frown on his face, and said, "Hi Rosie. It looks for all the world like a cat."

"Now isn't this the prettiest cat you ever saw?" Rosie answered. "Her name is Preacher Puss, and she's applied for a job here in the office as our mascot."

Bert got a stunned look on his face and said, "Rosie, I find that hard to believe. You better tell me the full story."

So Rosie told the sheriff everything she knew about me, and then looked at Bert with pleading eyes that begged for his approval.

He replied, "Rosie, cats are only good for catching mice, and we don't have that problem here in the office. Why would we want to put up with a cat?"

"Because I love her," Rosie replied. "And I would be personally responsible for her. I would go to the Wal-Mart and get all the supplies she would need, and I'd pay for those myself. She wouldn't cost the taxpayers one red cent."

I looked at the sheriff with my most appealing look. I slowly blinked my eyes and uttered a very long and mournful meow. How could he resist me?

The sheriff looked directly at me and then thought for a minute. He then said, "Rosie, I know you are a true animal lover. And I know you mean what you say about caring for the cat. Also, I know you must get a little bored sometimes here in the office when everything's quiet. I guess the cat could provide you some company, and that would be good for the office. So, okay. I guess we now have a special deputy named Preacher Puss." He then reached down and petted me, and I started my motor running big time, with a loud purr.

So that's the story of how I came to be here in the sheriff's office. But there's a lot more to tell! And I look forward to sharing it with you!

But before we get to some of my other adventures I should probably tell you a little about my situation here in the sheriff's office. On the day of my arrival Rosie did go to the Wal-Mart and purchased several goodies for me. She bought a very nice and comfortable bed, which she placed in the corner of the office behind her desk. She also got food and water bowls, and placed those beside my bed. And being the good-hearted soul that she is, she purchased a good supply of premium food and whisker-lickin cat treats. How she knew I loved those whisker-likin treats I really don't know, but that's what she got, and I sure am thankful. She also bought me several toys to play with, and they're okay, but I am, after all, now an adult cat and not a kitten. But it was good of her to think I might enjoy them, so mostly to please her I swat them around the office occasionally.

Also, when I arrived at the office there was another deputy that had a desk in the front office with Rosie. His name was Ape Cornett. I learned that Ape got his nickname due to his long arms and large hands. He was very thin and had been a deputy for Sheriff Sterling for about 15 years. Ape's desk was beside the entrance door. It was a good spot for me to jump on and watch what was going on in the office. One day I was leisurely sitting on Ape's desk when he decided to clean his pistol. He pulled the gun out of its holster and held it out in his right hand. My previous experience with a pistol kicked-in, and I immediately jumped from his desk onto his outstretched right arm with my claws extended. Upon impact with his arm the claws dug in deep. Ape screamed in pain, and immediately dropped his pistol to the floor. When that happened I withdrew my claws and jumped back on his desk and curled up for my nap. Rosie came running over to see what was the problem. She said, "Ape, you've got blood running from your arm. What happened?"

Ape replied, "I'm not real sure. I was just getting ready to clean my gun when Preacher Puss jumped onto my arms and clawed me pretty good. When the gun dropped to the floor she jumped back on my desk, and as you can see is now all content and taking a nap. Crazy."

Rosie said, "It sure is. But I think if I were you I'd clean my gun in the back where Preacher Puss can't see you. It seems like she doesn't like guns for some reason. That is strange."

I heard what they were saying, and I agreed with their conclusion. I don't like guns at all. And many times after that incident bad guys would come into the office and draw a gun and I'd be on 'em so fast they didn't know what hit 'em. So I gained quite a reputation for keeping peace in the sheriff's office. Sheriff Sterling liked to brag about how no one could draw a gun in his office.....deputy Preacher Puss was on the job!

Ape and I became real good friends, despite the shaky start. Soon after I got here he built me a shelf above the front door where I could lay and watch everything that was going on. Being a cat, I love high places, and I would jump from the floor to Ape's desk, and then from his desk up to the shelf above the door.

Rosie put a blanket on the shelf and I would lay there for hours on end cat napping and watching everything happening in the office. I loved it.

Well, that's a little of my history. I've been a member of the sheriff's staff now for about 17 years, and as near as I can figure I'm about 18 years old. That's pretty old for a cat, but I still feel pretty spry, and arthritis hasn't yet set in. I can still jump to the shelf above the entrance door, and I can run fast. My waist line has increased a bit, weighing in at 18 pounds on my last trip to the vet, but I was pronounced in remarkable shape for my age. I attribute most of that to the good life I've lived here in the sheriff's office and to Rosie's constant love and care. I'm very grateful.

Since my early days in the sheriff's office there have been several changes. Deputy Ape Cornett decided a few years ago that he wanted to pursue a career with the Kentucky State Police. He hated to leave the sheriff's department. He loved Sheriff Sterling and all the others in the office, but his heart was set on a career as a state trooper. After he departed, Sheriff Sterling appointed Kyle Potter to replace Ape as his chief deputy. Kyle is a remarkable young man. He is a native of Harlan and attended college at Eastern Kentucky University and received a degree in law enforcement. Sheriff Sterling had known Kyle all his life and was well aware of his remarkable abilities. Also, Kyle's mom, Carolyn, and Bert are very close friends. As a young boy Kyle had stumbled across a most historic and mysterious artifact one day as he roamed in the woods. But I'll tell you more about that later.

CHAPTER 2
PYONGYANG, NORTH KOREA

Kim Jong-un, the 3rd Supreme Leader of North Korea, dubbed "Little Rocket Man" by the U.S. President, sat at his desk. His face was crimson. He was furious. He had attempted several missions against the United States, and all had failed. He did not tolerate failure well. He thought about his initial attempt to steal the six mysterious, powerful anchor cross artifacts . . .

•••

In 325 AD Constantine the Great was emperor of Rome. He had converted to Christianity after being influenced greatly by his mother, Helena. Constantine had a dream, and in this dream he had a vision of a beautiful golden anchor cross that would symbolize the Christian religion. Prior to this time, and going back many centuries before Christ, the anchor was frequently used as a religious symbol. Hebrews 6:19 says, "We have this hope (meaning salvation through Christ) as an anchor of the soul, sure and steadfast." Until the time of Constantine the cross on which Christ was crucified was thought of in very negative terms because upon it only the worst criminals were placed. Perhaps in his vision Constantine was reminded of First Corinthians 1:18 that says, "For the message of the cross is foolishness to those who are perishing, but to us who are being saved it is the power of God." Constantine decided to share his vision with Pope Sylvester I who then told the emperor that he would give him a bar of very special gold from which he could mold his envisioned anchor cross. The bar of gold was one of many that had been blessed by the Lord and then given to Saint Peter to be used in establishing the church. It was called Saint Peter's gold. Constantine then gathered his most skilled craftsmen, described to them his anchor cross vision, and directed them to produce a mold which could be used to cast the golden anchor cross. This was done, and the result was a beautiful anchor cross about six inches high, four inches wide, and about one-half inch thick. The one bar of Saint Peter's gold was enough to produce six of the anchor crosses. Each had a hole in the top of the vertical arm of the cross that enabled a necklace to be threaded through so it could be worn about the neck.

Also, on the horizontal arm was formed the words *Pax Tecum*, Latin meaning "Peace be with you", a message from the one whom had blessed the gold, the Prince of Peace. The six anchor crosses were beautiful beyond belief. Constantine was delighted, and decided to keep one of them for himself and give the other five to Pope Sylvester I for the church to use as it decided appropriate.

Almost 17 years ago one of these anchor crosses was discovered in a remote location in the mountains of Eastern Kentucky by a child exploring in the woods. The boy, whose name was Kyle Potter, happened upon the ruins of a horse drawn wagon that had belonged to an early Harlan County, Kentucky pioneer named Reverend Karl Seibert, who, along with his wife Mary, were on their way in 1798 to the settlement called Mount Pleasant (later named Harlan) to start a church. The Seiberts had been attacked and killed by indians. Among the remains Kyle Potter recovered one of the golden anchor crosses. After showing the artifact to his mother she contacted their pastor, Raymond Bell, and he in turn contacted his friend in Lexington, Kentucky, Dr. Randy Peters, the Director of the University of Kentucky's Center for Appalachian Research. Dr. Peters uncovered the history of the artifact, now being called the Seibert anchor cross, and discovered that there were five more that Constantine had produced. Then, after another 12 years, the second anchor cross was discovered in Prato, Italy where it had been placed in a church by its wealthy owner, Mr. Domenico Pelle. The remaining anchor crosses then began being discovered around the world. The third, the Helena anchor cross, was found in the Seychelles, the fourth and fifth were located in Madrid, Spain and were owned by twin sisters Elisabeth and Henriette Carmen, descendents in the lineage of French King Louis XV. The sixth and final anchor cross, the one that Constantine kept for himself, was found about 18 months ago by treasurer hunters diving off the Italian coast close to the island of Ponza. Having established himself as the world's leading authority on the anchor crosses, also called the Savior's crosses, Dr. Randy Peters had temporary possession of all six of the artifacts at his Lexington, Kentucky Center for Appalachian Research (CAR). The owners of the artifacts had all agreed to allow Dr. Peters to study them in an attempt to better understand their amazing history and characteristics. Each of the six anchor crosses had demonstrated numerous times amazing, unexplained power to protect from harm those possessing them. The media had reported world-wide the stories of each of these Savior's crosses, and their fame had even resulted in an annual October festival held in Harlan, Kentucky in their honor. The festival was called ACFes. Thousands flooded the streets of Harlan each year to view and celebrate the beautiful golden artifacts.

It was their world-wide media coverage that came to the attention of North Korea Supreme Leader Kim Jong-un. Kim was not impressed by their history, beauty, or their value. He was intrigued by the mysterious power they seemed to possess. He had a team of researchers study what was known about the artifacts, and after hearing that each anchor cross had indeed exhibited unexplained power to protect the wearer he commissioned a team of six of his best military people to travel to the United States with the mission to steal all six anchor crosses during their exhibition at the annual ACFes in Harlan, Kentucky. Kim was then prepared to send the team of six to Washington, D.C. to capture the White House and thus give him power over the U.S. Each man would be wearing one of the anchor crosses for protection, and therefore should be unstoppable to accomplish the mission. But when the soldiers attempted the theft, an unexpected event occurred that aborted their mission. Kim was furious, and executed many in his government that he held responsible for the failed attempt. The six North Koreans involved in the plot were taken under the wing of Harlan County Sheriff J. Bert Sterling. The sheriff recognized that the six were merely serving their despicable dictator, and that they would be executed if returned to North Korea. Also, Sheriff Sterling sensed that the six were basically very good people, just misdirected. So he managed to place them with two brothers, the Slusher Brothers, who agreed to allow them to work on their large Harlan County farm while their applications for political asylum were being processed.

Kim had then sent one of his top Generals to Harlan County having as his mission to kill all the deserters now living at the Slusher farm. This attempt also resulted in failure, and the General wound up being accepted by the Slusher Brothers and joined his comrades working happily at their farm, having been granted political asylum.

But then the crowning blow to Kim came just a few months ago when he decided that for his birthday he would have a nuclear bomb dropped on Los Angeles. He sent a team of soldiers to commandeer a civilian container vessel in a scheme to get the ship close enough to the U.S. west coast to fire a Soviet cruise-type missile with a nuclear warhead. American intelligence uncovered the plot, and located an Ex-North Korean General recently granted political asylum and living at the Slusher Brothers farm to undertake the very dangerous mission that successfully aborted the attack.

•••

These failures were just more than Kim could tolerate. He felt he absolutely had to get revenge..... he would be satisfied with nothing less than a successful mission that would deliver a blow to the Slusher Brothers' farm that would kill all of the North Korean deserters, the Slusher Brothers, and anyone else unfortunate enough to be there when the strike occurred. He had thought of virtually nothing else since his attempted nuclear strike failed. He now had in mind exactly how he would get even. His red face slowly returned to its normal color, and a smile began to form. "Sweet revenge," he thought. "Sweet, sweet revenge will be mine!"

CHAPTER 3
HARLAN, KENTUCKY

"Bert, I'm really excited about my upcoming vacation trip. I'm just so looking forward to spending some time with my mother in Tennessee.," Rosie said. "My husband couldn't get off work, but he encouraged me to go. He knew how happy my mother would be to have me visit with her."

Sheriff Sterling replied, "Well, Rosie, you've certainly more than earned your time off. We'll struggle to get along without you, and especially without Preacher Puss!" The sheriff had a smile on his face.

"Yeah, I know you'll miss her. But I just have to take her along with me. If she wasn't along I'd worry the whole time I was gone, and the vacation would be spoiled. Plus, I really think she'll enjoy the trip. As you know, Mom lives in the country, so ole Preacher Puss will be able to get outdoors and explore around. She'll love it."

They were both now looking at me. I heard every word they said. I was lying on my shelf above the entrance door, and had been taking a cat nap, but when they started with the vacation talk it got my attention. I slowly began to swish my tail and opened one eye looking at them. This vacation thing sounded pretty good, although I don't have any idea where this 'Tennessee' is, and I haven't met Rosie's mom. But I'm sure she would be nice, like Rosie. And it would be good to get out of the office for a while.

"See there," Rosie said. "She's swishing her tail. She knows we're talking about her....and I bet she even knows she's getting ready to go on vacation."

Bert laughed and replied, "Yeah, that cat seems almost human. I do think she understands a lot of things that we don't give her credit for. My only problem is that with her out of the office I just won't feel as safe and secure. But I guess I can get along without the two of you for a week."

Rosie said, "I'm sure you and the office will be just fine during our absence. And I know that my sister Posey will take care of all my duties next week." Posey normally filled in for Rosie anytime she had to be off work. Sheriff Sterling had made Posey a deputy sheriff several years ago so that she might substitute for Rosie. "We leave first thing in the morning. It's Saturday, so I hope the traffic won't be too bad. I have your cell phone number, so if I have any problems I'll let you know,"

Bert leaned forward and gave Rosie a peck on her cheek, and then walked over to me and gave me a nice pet. He said, "You two take care, and I'll see you a week from Monday."

• • •

Rosie and I had been driving for about two hours. We left Harlan on highway 119 to Pineville, then took highway 25E to Harrogate, Tennessee, and then highway 63 to LaFollette/Caryville where we got on interstate 75 headed South toward Knoxville. We had been on the interstate for about 15 minutes when we started to hear a "thump, thump, thump" noise coming from the back of our car. There was a nice wide shoulder, so Rosie pulled well off the road and brought the car to a stop.

"Well Preacher Puss, it sounds like we might have a flat tire!"

Rosie got out and looked at both rear tires. "Yep, that left rear is flat as a flitter," she said. "Guess I'd better get the jack out and try to get the spare on."

After stopping, Rosie had rolled down all the car windows. I jumped up on the top of the back seat and had a good view of everything, looking out the back and side windows. I felt sorry for Rosie, but there's just some things a cat can't do, and helping change a flat tire is one of them.

Just as she was removing the jack from the car's trunk another car pulled in behind us. A fellow got out and walked up to Rosie and said, "Hi Missy, looks like you got yourself a flat tire. Maybe I could help you!" I didn't like the looks of this guy. He had long stringy hair and a beard that was badly in need of a razor. He was tall and skinny, and I would judge him to be about 30 years old. He was wearing jeans and a T-shirt that looked to me like they had seen their better days.

"Well . . . I could probably handle it," Rosie replied. "But if you really want to help I'd certainly appreciate it."

"Sure thing," the guy said. "You just sit your pretty self down in the car and I'll take care of everything."

Rosie slowly moved to the driver's seat and sat. The guy started to jack up the rear of the car. After about a minute the motion of the car stopped, and it was then that I saw the guy reach into his pocket and remove a pistol. He was holding it with his right hand and started moving forward toward the driver's door and Rosie. I felt duty call! The man was squatted down, moving slowly toward Rosie with a gun extended forward in his right hand . As his head passed just beneath the left rear window I sprung from my perch on the back seat through the window with all four of my paws below me, claws extended, and landed directly atop his head. The claws dug in deeply. The man screamed in agony, as blood started gushing down his face. He dropped his gun and reached for me with both hands.

That's when Rosie quickly opened her door, jumped out of the car, and slammed her knee up into the guys private parts. His screams got much louder as he fell to the ground. I jumped back in the car and back to my viewing perch on the top of the back seat. I knew Rosie had everything well in hand. She quickly pulled a set of handcuffs from the glove box, pulled the man's hands behind his back, and fastened the handcuffs on him. He was lying prone on the ground, blood still streaming down his face, and still screaming in pain.

Rosie said, "Scream all you like, I'm calling 911 for help." Rosie grabbed both her cell phone and a can of mace. She had one foot on the back of the man's head and pointed the mace nozzle toward his head. "You try to get up and I'm using this mace."

Just as she was starting to dial 911 a Tennessee state trooper pulled in behind the two cars with his flasher going. He jumped out of his car and started running toward Rosie and the would-be robber. When he saw Rosie with the mace pointed toward the handcuffed guy on the ground with a bloody head he started to withdraw his revolver.

"No, no, no . . . don't pull your gun!! My cat will attack you!" Rosie screamed at the trooper.

He kept his hand on the gun handle, but eased the gun back in its holster. He had a somewhat puzzled look on his face as he said, "Lady, I'm a little confused about what we have here. Perhaps you'd best explain."

Rosie couldn't help but smile, and then she told the officer exactly what had happened, and that she was a deputy sheriff from Harlan County, Kentucky on vacation with her cat headed for Knoxville.

"That's some cat you've got there," the trooper said as he jerked the robber to his feet.

"She's the pride of the Harlan County Sheriff's office," replied Rosie. I beamed with satisfaction, and acknowledged with a reassuring meow.

After administering first-aid and exchanging his handcuffs for Rosie's, the trooper secured the robber in the back of his cruiser. He then called for a wrecker to transport the bad guy's car to impound, after which he walked back up to Rosie's car and said, "Lady, you and that cat seemed to take care of everything very nicely. I'll just need to fill out a report, then I'll put your spare tire on, and we can both be on our way. I can't wait to tell everyone at my headquarters about this incident, and especially about ole Preacher Puss." He then reached back and gave me a nice, gentle pet which I acknowledged with a purr and a large swish of my tail.

The flat fixed, Rosie honked the horn and waved good-bye to the helpful trooper, and we carefully pulled back onto I75. Rosie's mother was really going to enjoy hearing this story.

CHAPTER 4
PYONGYANG, NORTH KOREA

The supreme leader was obviously very intense. He was sitting at his desk with the commander of his air force, General Ri Pyong-rok, standing at attention before him.

Kim Jong-un said, "General Ri, I want to make absolutely certain you understand what I demand. I demand that the three men you recommend to me are the very best helicopter pilots in the Korean People's Army Air Force. The mission I have for them is crucial for our country. Failure by them will result in very severe repercussions to you and others responsible for their recommendation. Do you understand me?"

"Yes, Supreme Leader," replied General Ri. "There is no doubt about these three men. I personally know each of them, and I've had them very thoroughly examined. They will fulfill your mission with excellence."

"They better," Kim replied. "What are their names?"

"Colonel Lee Gum-Jun, Colonel Gim Eun-Jung, and Colonel Yie Byung-Ho," replied General Ri. "These are our absolutely best helicopter pilots, and they will serve the supreme leader with their lives. They are anxious for the mission."

"And I understand that they do speak and understand English," replied Kim.

"Yes," said General Ri, "They have had extensive training in both the English language and culture. They will not have any problem functioning in the United States."

Kim said, "Okay, I want you to do two things as you leave. Tell my secretary to schedule you and the three pilots for a meeting with me at 3 pm this afternoon, and tell her I'm ready for my mid-morning snack. I want three egg-McMuffins, two orders of pancakes, and coffee. Got that?"

"Yes, supreme leader. It shall be done," replied General Ri as he turned and walked out of Kim's office.

Kim was addicted to McDonald's foods. While a student in Switzerland he frequented the McDonalds restaurant there and grew very fond of all their foods. After becoming supreme leader he commissioned a team of North Korean cooks to go to Switzerland with the mission of learning McDonald's menu and upon their return to Pyongyang to be able to reproduce it for him. They stayed in Switzerland four weeks to accomplish this, and each gained 12 pounds. Kim loved to eat. He was 5 feet, 5 inches tall and weighed 330 pounds. He suffered from gout, and had a difficult time walking.

•••

SAME DAY, 3 pm

Kim sat at his desk. He had just finished a large Chocolate Milk Shake, and was now starting on another one. Sitting on a couch to Kim's right was General Ri. Three soldiers stood at attention before his desk.

Kim said, "Colonels Lee, Gim, and Yie. I have read your personnel folders, and I have discussed your qualifications with General Ri. You come highly recommended for this mission. I must tell you that I will be satisfied with nothing less than total success. Do you understand?"

"Yes, supreme leader," the three said in unison.

"You better," Kim replied. "Now I want to tell you exactly what you are expected to accomplish.

You will be provided with all necessary documents and western dress for your misssion. You will fly to Atlanta, Georgia in the United States, and will rent a car at the airport. You will then drive to Knoxville, Tennessee and meet with a man named Maggard. His address will be provided to you. Mr. Maggard will have accommodations for you, and you will stay with him for a couple of days. He will procure a helicopter for you. It will be a Robinson R22 Beta II, which I'm told you are familiar. It is a very light weight helicopter that can carry 400 pounds plus 157 pounds of fuel. For your mission you will only require about 50 pounds of fuel, so that leaves about 500 pounds for pilots and cargo. You each weigh about 160 pounds. Two pilots will then be 320 pounds, leaving about 180 pounds for cargo. Your cargo will be two bombs, each weighing approximately 75 pounds. Each will be capable of completely destroying the building you will be dropping them on, but by dropping two we will have a good factor of safety. The target will be utterly obliterated. Nothing will be left standing, or alive. Do you understand?"

The three pilots looked at each other, and then Colonel Lee said, "Yes, supreme leader, we understand. Could we ask where and what is the target, and how we and the helicopter will get there?"

"Ah, good questions," Kim replied. "The target is a farm house in Harlan County, Kentucky. It is about 100 miles from where you will be staying with Mr. Maggard in Knoxville, Tennessee. Mr. Maggard will procure a semi-trailer and the helicopter will be loaded in the totally enclosed trailer. The helicopter's length is 28 feet, it's width is just over 6 feet, and it's height is 9 feet. It was chosen because it can be transported inside a semi-trailer. It's my understanding that the three of you have experience in driving such a truck and trailer, and there should be room for all three of you in the truck cab."

Colonel Lee replied, "Yes, we are familiar with such trucks, and that should be no problem. Could I also ask where we will be taking the truck and helicopter?"

"Certainly," Kim said. "Mr. Maggard will have made arrangements with a person owning a small farm where you will take the helicopter. He will give you the directions after you arrive in Knoxville. This farm is in a very remote area, across a large mountain from the target. As the crow flies, the distance you'll have to fly to the target will only be a few miles, but it'll be over a mountain with no roads or trails directly between the two. Mr. Maggard has paid and made arrangements with the farm owner for him to leave on vacation just as soon as you arrive with the truck and helicopter. The farm will be deserted except for you three, and you'll be able to stay in the farm house until the day of the mission."

"Yes, supreme leader, everything sounds very good," said Colonel Lee with the other two pilots nodding in agreement.

CHAPTER 5
NEAR KNOXVILLE, TENNESSEE

Rosie and I had taken exit 108 from interstate 75, just North of Knoxville. We had turned left onto Cedar Lane and proceeded a couple of miles before coming to her mother's home. It was in a rural setting, with lots of trees all around. Rosie had told me that her mom's home was on a 5 acre lot, and that I'd be allowed to roam around on it so long as I promised not to go too far. Believe me, after my experience leaving the Slusher farm she certainly didn't have to worry about that. But it did sound very inviting, and I looked forward greatly to exploring.

Upon arrival, Rosie's mom was waiting in the driveway to greet us. Rosie had called her when she exited the interstate to let her know we were about there. I understand Rosie's mom's real name is Martha Jane, but of course Rosie just calls her mom.

"Welcome, welcome, welcome," mom said. "I've been so excited about your visit that I didn't sleep well last night. I hope you had a good trip."

"Hi mom," Rosie replied. "It is so good to see you," she said as she got out of the car and gave her mother a big hug and kiss. "Except for one little blip, we did have a good trip. I'll tell you about it later. But right now I want you to meet Preacher Puss." She reached into the back seat and gently lifted me in her arms out of the car.

I looked at mom and let out my best meow, along with a long, gentle swish of my tail.

"Now isn't that the prettiest cat I ever saw," mom replied as she petted gently on my head. "Preacher Puss, your reputation preceeds you! Rosie has keep me posted on all your adventures, and I'm deeply honored to meet you."

Times like this I truly wish I could smile, but I think mom did catch the twinkle in my eye. I just love getting praise. Mom and I are going to get along real good!

After unpacking the car and getting all settled in mom said, "Okay, now that we've got you all settled I want to show Preacher Puss her living quarters."

My ears perked up . . . I'm going to have living quarters!! Oh boy!!

Mom said, "You two follow me." She lead us toward the garage. Her home is a ranch, and on one end is the garage. There is a door going into the garage from the kitchen. We all walked into the garage. It was large enough for two cars, but only mom's car was in it. In the other car space she had placed a nice cat bed, and beside it a bowl containing water and one containing my favorite cat food. As she pointed these out she said, "Now Preacher Puss, Rosie told me about how you enjoy napping up high. So, if you look over there beside the door you'll see that I have a shelf all cleaned out and have placed a cuddly blanket on it. You are most welcome to jump up there and enjoy some cat naps. I bet you can jump up there by first jumping on the washer and then on up to the shelf. How do you like it?"

I responded by quickly jumping on the washer and then on up to the shelf. I laid down on the blanket, looked down on the two ladies, and gave a big, approval purr.

"How about that, mom," Rosie said. "I think Preacher Puss just thanked you."

"Well, she's very welcome," mom replied. "I just hope she'll be comfortable in here. At my age I was concerned that when I got up at night to go to the bathroom she might accidently get under my feet causing me to fall. So I thought it'd be best if at night she slept here in the garage. Do you think she'll mind?"

"Not at all," Rosie said. "I think she understands, and I know she'll be comfortable here. If you don't mind maybe we could leave the garage door propped up enough so that she could go outside whenever she wanted."

Mom said, "No problem. As you know my garage door is manual, so we can just prop the door up with a box large enough to let her go in and out."

I meowed largely my approval. This was really going to be a fun visit!

Rosie and I were both a little tired from our trip, so we just hung around the house with mom the rest of the day. I would perch where ever convenient and listen to the two of them talk. Rosie told her all about our encounter with the bad guy on our way here, and she made me the hero of the story. I really liked that. And I listened to all their other conversations. They had a lot of catching up to do.

After dinner Rosie said to me, "Preacher Puss, you haven't explored outside at all. I thought you'd likely do that as soon as we got here."

I guess she didn't realize that I was a little tired from the trip too. I just looked at her.

"Well, you'll have plenty of time for that. We'll be here for the next week!" she said.

I meowed in reply.

Later that evening Rosie carried me to the garage, and after propping the garage door open with a small box she told me good-night. She reached into her dress pocket and pulled out two whisker-lickin treats and laid them on my food bowl. I knew immediately what they were and responded with a big, thankful tail swish and meow. She then gave me a nice pet and walked out of the garage, closing the door going into the kitchen.

I had two choices for sleeping. One, I could sleep in the nice cat bed that mom had provided beside my food and water bowls on the floor, or two, I could jump up on the shelf and sleep on the blanket there. It's nice to have choices! I knew I'd wind up using both of them, so I thought I'd first try the bed on the floor. I got in, fluffed up the blanket in it, and then curled up on it. I was asleep in a flash.

I had slept for a few hours when all of a sudden I awoke. I slowly and carefully opened one eye. I had heard some kind of strange noise....it sounded like something 'swishing' on the floor. I then opened both eyes and very slowly started turning my head toward the noise. There was some light in the garage, coming in through the windows and from the crack under the propped up garage door. Not a lot, but then us cats don't need a lot of light to see! It was then that I saw the outline of something moving between me and the garage door. It was definitely there, but I couldn't tell what it was. It moved very slowly, and it was coming toward me! I was scared! My fur started to straighten, and my claws began to extend. I lowered my head and focused as best I could on the intruder. I was ready to pounce.

It moved closer. Then, all of a sudden, it's face moved into a beam of light coming from one of the windows. That's when I saw it!! It looked for all the world like a robber. It looked like it was wearing a mask, and it had big eyes that were staring straight back at me. It was about my size, and was furry, but it definitely was not a cat. I had never seen anything like it before. I was really, really scared now. But I had to defend myself!

I bared my teeth and took a swat toward it with my right paw, with claws extended. I was hoping that might scare it off. It didn't. The thing stood up on its hind feet and started making swatting motions at me with its front feet. It looked like an encounter was not to be avoided.

I then very slowly started to rise to my feet, just moving ever so slowly. I stayed in a low, crouched position and kept my eyes focused directly on it.

It then leaped and tried to get on top of me. I swatted back with both front paws as I tried to raise up on my back feet. I felt it's claws on my back, and I'm sure it felt mine dug into its tummy. It then tried to bite my tail, and I returned the favor. My teeth sunk into its swishing tail. We both screamed out and then started to roll around on the garage floor clawing at each other.

The door going to the kitchen opened, and Rosie and her mom came running into the garage. They turned the light on, and saw the two animals wrestling on the floor.

Mom said, "Rosie, that's a raccoon fighting Preacher Puss. What can we do?"

Rosie looked in the corner of the garage and saw a water hose. She ran over to it, turned on the water valve, and started spraying us with water. Now let me tell you that cats do not like water. And apparently these things called raccoons don't either. We both immediately quit fighting and started to run away from the water spray. I went to one corner of the garage, and the raccoon to another. Then Rosie turned the water hose toward the raccoon, and it quickly started running toward the propped up garage door. It went under the door and escaped outside.

Rosie put the hose down and ran over to me. She grabbed a towel from the laundry basket and put it around me as she lifted me up. "You poor kitty. That mean ole coon sneaked in here and attacked you. Are you okay?"

I wanted to say yes, but a little scratched up. Rosie examined me and apparently arrived at that conclusion.

"Mom, I'm going to put some antiseptic on these scratches, and then if they look bad tomorrow we'll take Preacher Puss to the vet. They don't look too bad to me....hopefully she'll be just fine."

Mom replied, "That coon sure scared me. I guess we put the garage door down. We wouldn't want him to come back."

"Yeah, I guess we'll have to," Rosie replied. "I'll open it again tomorrow during the daytime so she can go out to explore. We'll just have to start leaving it closed at night."

After drying me off with the towel and administering the first-aid, Rosie put me back in my bed and bid me another good-night. I sure hoped this one would work better than the last!

CHAPTER 6
KNOXVILLE, TENNESSEE

Pretty Boy Maggard currently lives in Knoxville, Tennessee. Prior to that he had lived in Harlan County, Kentucky. He had owned a small grocery store, Maggard's Grocery, located a few miles south of Harlan on highway 119, near the town of Wallins. Pretty Boy was a crook. When he owned Maggard's Grocery he used it only as a front for his illegal operations. He was into about anything that would make him a buck, i.e. moonshine, drugs, making book, bootlegging, credit card theft and scams, robbery, fencing stolen goods, etc. All of these operations he directed out of an office in the back of the grocery. The front part was set up as a small grocery store, and he had a clerk named Fatso Chapel that looked after the grocery store. Fatso usually just sat at the cash register and either read magazines and books or watched a small tv that sat beside the register. Fatso loved to tell corny jokes. Most of those that knew him tried to avoid him because of them. But about 17 years ago Pretty Boy

Richard G. Edwards

got caught fencing several million dollars of illegal drug money. He escaped to Columbia, and then after a few years moved to Knoxville, Tennessee, and was never caught. He sold his grocery store to his number one assistant in crime, Trigger Green. Trigger reopened the store, kept the Maggard name, and kept Fatso Chapel to run the grocery operation while he continued with all the illegal operations from his office in the back of the store. Trigger was very smart, and could carry out his illegal activity most of the time without getting caught. But unlike Pretty Boy Maggard, Trigger Green had a good heart, and often times had cooperated with Sheriff Sterling to catch crooks that operated beyond his limits. Trigger certainly was a crook, but he was a 'good crook'.

Pretty Boy had purchased a small junk yard in Knoxville, and spent his time using it as a front for lots of illegal activity. He had connections with drug lords in Columbia, and through them had made other connections worldwide. Through this network Kim Jong-un had sent him instructions and money to help the three air force pilots with their plan to bomb the Slusher farm house in Harlan County, Kentucky. Kim had provided Pretty Boy with enough money to purchase (1) 150 pounds of extremely high energy explosives, (2) a Robinson R22 Beta II helicopter, (3) a used semi-truck large enough to carry the helicopter, and $25,000 to give to the pilots for use as needed. He had also given him an additional $200,000 for his fee. Pretty Boy was responsible for keeping the pilots at his home until they were ready to drive the semi to Harlan County, to arrange for them to get a car after arriving there, and to provide them with detailed instructions and maps. Kim had also worked with Pretty Boy to find and rent a remote farm in Harlan County from which they would operate. This farm was only a few miles from their target, but was across a mountain range without any direct roads between the two farms. Pretty Boy had known the owner of the farm when he previously lived in Harlan County, and had contacted him and made arrangements to rent the farm for two weeks for $50,000.....no questions asked. The owner agreed, and said he would take off on vacation to Florida for the two week period. Everything was all set!

"I don't see why we have to go look at it again," said Pretty Boy. "You guys have gone over it with a fine tooth comb several times. Why do we need to see it again today?"

Pretty Boy was walking beside Colonel Lee. Colonels Gim and Yie followed behind them. They were walking toward an old barn that was on Pretty Boy's junk yard property. The three pilots had arrived in Knoxville three days ago. Pretty Boy had returned their rental car, and then spent most of his time the last three days going over the plans for them to get the semi to Harlan County.

"Just this one last check," said Colonel Lee. "We want to make sure that the helicopter skids will properly accommodate the bomb package. We appreciate your patience with us."

Pretty Boy replied, "Well, I thought we'd gone over all that, but okay, we'll check it out."

The foursome arrived at the old barn. Pretty Boy removed the key ring from his belt, and unlocked the barn door. They then opened the two large doors, walked inside, and turned on the overhead lights. Colonel Lee then took a key that Pretty Boy had given him, and used it to unlock the rear doors on the semi-trailer, and then opened them. Inside, sitting on a large wooden pallet, was the Robinson helicopter. The two bomb packages were sitting on the floor of the semi, and secured firmly to the front of the wooden pallet, one on each front side. The pallet had only a couple of inches clearance along its sides, and thus prevented lateral movement of the helicopter while the truck was in motion. A single wooden brace fastened to the pallet fore and aft prevented it from sliding in those directions.

Colonel Lee jumped up into the rear of the semi. He then looped the end of a rope attached to one of the bombs around the right front helicopter skid, and did the same with the one on the left. Each of these ropes had a metal box located midway between their ends. After doing this he extracted a small remote control from his pocket, looked at the men standing on the ground looking up at him, smiled and said, "Okay, here goes the test." He then pushed the red button on the remote control.

The metal boxes located midway on both ropes immediately released the rope on their bottom end, and the ropes fell back onto the bomb packages.

"Success!" said Colonel Lee. "We just wanted to test these actuators before we go on the mission. Their function in dropping the bombs is critical. They passed the test."

"I knew they'd work fine," responded Pretty Boy. "I checked them out myself several times. The guy I had make 'em knows what he's doing."

After securing the semi and the barn, the four returned to Pretty Boy's office.

All four got a cup of coffee and then took a seat around an old table. Pretty Boy said, "I know we've gone over everything several times, but this will be your last chance to ask me any questions. You leave in the morning for Harlan County."

Colonel Lee said, "Please allow me to go over our plans one last time. The three of us will depart driving the semi tomorrow morning at 8 am. We will get on highway 33 going north. When we arrive at a town called Tazewell, we take highway 25E going north. We pass into Kentucky and after about 15 miles come to the town of Pineville where we take highway 119 north toward the town of Harlan. About a mile after we come to a road marked 'to Wallins' we will see a grocery store on our right, with a sign that says 'Maggard's Grocery'. Your old store, Mr. Maggard," Lee said with a smile, "after parking I go into the store and meet a gentleman named Fatso Chapel. I tell him I would like to see Mr. Green. Mr. Green will then give me the keys to a car that will be parked in the front of the store. Colonels Gim and Yie will then get back in the truck, and I will drive the car. The truck will then follow me to the farm where we will be staying. I will carefully follow my directions. I drive near to the town of Harlan, and at the intersection with highway 421 I turn left and follow this route across a mountain called Pine. After crossing the mountain I turn right on route 221 and proceed for about 5 miles. I will then come to a dirt road on the right with a mail box having the name 'Stepp' on it. The mail box post will also have a red ribbon tied around it and made into a big red bow. I turn onto that road and drive about one half mile to the farm house. We will park the semi beside the farm barn, and then get settled in the house. The house will be empty and unlocked."

Pretty Boy smiled and thought, these boys are strange, but very smart. He then said, "You got it. Just follow those directions and everything should go smooth as silk. You boys now need to get a good day's rest, a good night's sleep, and be all ready to go first thing in the morning. I'm not sure what your mission is, other than to drop those bombs somewhere, but I wish you luck. I'll be looking to see you back here after its completed, and I'll get you a rental car to drive back to the Atlanta airport. You have my cell phone number if you need me."

All three pilots nodded in agreement. Colonel Lee then said, "Thank you Mr. Maggard. You have been very helpful. I think all will go well."

CHAPTER 7
KNOXVILLE, TENNESSEE

Yesterday Rosie and I got pretty much rested up, other than the disturbance last night by the animal called a raccoon. He sure looked like a robber, with those black rings around his eyes! But other than that, I got well rested and even slept a little late this morning. Rosie looked in on me around 9 am. I perked up when I saw the kitchen door to the garage open. Rosie came in and checked my scratches, and then proclaimed me good as new. She even rewarded me with several whisker-likin treats! Boy, this vacation thing is okay!!

She went over and propped the garage door open again wedging a small box between the floor and the bottom of the garage door. She said, "Preacher Puss, if you want to go outside and explore, feel free to do so. Just be sure you stay close and don't get into trouble."

I meowed in reply, and then followed her into the house through the kitchen door. She left it open so I could go back into the garage, and then outside if I wished.

After a few minutes visitation with mom and Rosie, I decided it was time for me to do a little exploring. I wanted to see what I might see in the woods surrounding the house. So I trotted back into the garage and under the propped up garage door out onto the driveway. I then walked slowly around to the back yard, carefully observing as I went. Things smelled different here. Everything smelled very fresh and woodsy. I decided just to sit for a minute and watch, just to see if I saw anything of interest. I did see several squirrels running on the overhead power lines and through the trees, but they didn't bother me and I didn't bother them. Looking straight back through the woods I couldn't see any other homes....just trees and shrub. So I started to slowly walk into it. There was a small dirt trail, and I followed it. I decided I couldn't get lost if I stayed on the path.

After walking for about 5 minutes down the trail I saw something in the bushes off to my left. I looked, and saw bushes and leaves moving. There was no breeze in here, so it wasn't the wind. I decided I'd try and find out what caused it. I walked about 25 feet off the path toward where I saw the movement. And then, all of a sudden, I wished I'd stayed on the trail! I had almost stepped on a snake! It was coiled up, and it's tail was stuck up in the air and made a rattling sound. I'd never seen one of these, but I'd heard people in the sheriff's office talk about rattle snakes, and how dangerous and mean they were. And now I'd found my very own!! I froze. It continued to make the noise with its tail. I knew I was close enough to it to be within its striking range, and I knew if I moved it would likely strike me. I didn't know what to do!

It was at that instant that I saw another animal of some kind moving up on the snake from the side opposite me. I had the snake's attention, and it didn't see the other animal, which was creeping slowly forward in a crouched position. It was then that I saw the animal's face....it was a raccoon! It looked exactly like the one that I encountered last night in the garage. When it got within a couple of feet of the snake it suddenly pounced onto the snake's head with it's claws. It looked like one claw went into one of the snake's eyes. The snake literally seemed to jump off the ground. The raccoon then bit the neck of the snake, and I saw some kind of liquid come from the puncture. As the raccoon then tried to get hold of the snake with both its front feet the snake quickly slithered out from under the raccoon and off into the brush. The fight was a standoff. Neither raccoon or snake won, but I quickly decided that the victory was mine! I didn't get bitten, and from what I had heard about rattlesnake bites, I could well have been a goner.

I looked at the raccoon with my best apologetic and thankful look. It looked at me with what seemed a curious look, although with those dark rings around its eyes it still looked for all the world like a bandit! I let out a very soft and inviting meow. I wanted the raccoon to know that I was thankful....it likely saved my life! We both just sat and looked at each other for a couple more minutes, neither of us moving a muscle. Finally the raccoon started to very slowly inch toward me. I really didn't think it wanted to fight or do me harm, so I just sat and waited. And then it did a very curious thing. When it got right next to me it started to lick one of my scratches that I got from the fight last night. It was then that I saw a puncture wound on its tail where I had bitten it, so I started to lick that wound. We both seemed to relax, and after a couple of licking moments, we both stopped and just sat beside each other like friends.

I guess Rosie and mom must have seen or heard the commotion, and they came running down the trail toward us. While they were still on the trail just off from us they looked our way. Rosie said, "Well, well.

Would you look at that! That raccoon is back, and it looks like it's made friends with Preacher Puss."

Mom looked and said, "Rosie, they do seem like friends now . . . just sitting there together. Maybe they made up."

"Sure does look like it," Rosie replied.

I then let out my best contented meow, loud and slow.

Rosie said, "I sure don't want any more fights. I've got a few whisker-likins here in my pocket. Maybe raccoons like 'em too." She held one out in her hand and then slowly started walking toward us. I knew she wanted to offer it to my new friend, so I restrained myself as it got close. The raccoon then raised up on its hind legs and reached for the treat with its front paws. It grabbed it, stuck it in its mouth, and chewed. Then it started sniffing all around like it was interested in more. So Rosie gave it two or three more, and it gobbled them down. Rosie then gave me one, which I graciously accepted.

"They are now friends," Rosie said to mom. "I just know it. They won't be fighting again."

"I sure hope you're right," replied mom. "We don't need any big vet bills."

"I think we should just let them be," Rosie replied.

"Let them enjoy their new found friendship."

The two ladies then turned and walked back to the house. My new friend and I started to sniff each other appropriately, and after a couple of minutes of sniffing, we trotted along together through the brush, seeing what we might find. We explored together for the next hour or so, and then wound up back at the house. We had bonded!! I led the way around the house to the garage, and entered through the propped up door. My new friend followed closely behind. When we got into the garage I jumped up to my blanket on the shelf, and my friend curled up in my bed on the floor. We were both tired, and immediately fell asleep.

Some time later the door between the kitchen and garage opened and Rosie and mom walked in. After spotting both of us mom said, "My, my! Would you look at that. Preacher Puss invited that coon back in the garage. I guess they truly must be buddies."

Rosie said, "For sure! Everything is peaceful now. I guess you've just got a new buddy too, mom. What are you going to name it?"

Mom replied, "I don't even know if it's a him or her, but I guess we could just call it 'Bandit'. With those rings around its eyes it seems an appropriate name."

"Bandit and Preacher Puss," Rosie said. "I'm glad

that's settled, and I'm glad ole Preacher Puss has a friend to play with during our visit!"

I didn't open my eyes, but I heard every word they said. I bet Bandit heard them too. This vacation thing just got a lot better!

CHAPTER 8
HARLAN COUNTY, KENTUCKY

It was a normal, quiet morning at Maggard's grocery. Fatso had just finished stocking a few items in the store, and had returned to his seat behind the cash register and began to read a magazine. The door bell jingled, and Fatso looked up to see Mrs. Cavanaugh entering the store.

"Good Morning Mrs. Cavanaugh," Fatso shouted. "I bet you need a few groceries this fine morning!"

"Morning Fatso," she replied. "Yes, my daughter's coming over for a visit this afternoon and I wanted to pick up a few snacks for us. Everything going well with you?"

"About normal," said Fatso. "Hey, Mrs. Cavanaugh, you know why more elephants don't go to college?"

She replied, "Well, I hadn't really given that any thought. But, no, I really don't. I bet you're going to tell me!"

"Very few elephants go to college because not many finish high school!" Fatso shouted with a chuckle.

"That's cute, Fatso, I always enjoy your corny jokes," she said as she continued her shopping.

•••

In the back room Trigger Green sat at his desk. His cell phone rang.

"Maggard's grocery, this is Trigger Green," he said.

"Good morning Trigger, this is Pretty Boy, how you doin?"

"Hey Pretty Boy, good to hear your voice. I'm good . . . you still in Knoxville?"

"Right here in Rocky Top Land," Pretty Boy replied. "I got a little business I need to discuss with you."

"Go right ahead, Pretty Boy. Business I can use."

Pretty Boy said, "Tomorrow sometime around 11 am a semi truck will pull into the parking lot at your store. There will be three guys in the truck cab. One will get out and come into the store. He's been instructed to tell Fatso he wants to talk with you. When he gets with you in your office he'll have an envelope containing $10,000 cash. In exchange, I want you to have a car waiting for him. It shouldn't be anything new or flashy, just a sedan of some kind maybe about 5 or 6 years old and some color that wouldn't draw attention. Maybe black, white, grey . . . something like that. And it should have current Harlan county tags and registration. I feel certain you can come up with something that fits that description that shouldn't cost you more than $5,000, if that much. The rest of the money is yours. You may or may not get the car back, it just depends on how things go. Think you can handle that?"

Trigger said, "Sounds like a piece of cake to me, Pretty Boy. I'll have the car parked out in front tomorrow morning by 10 am, and will be looking for that semi a little later. Just as soon as we hang up I'll call a guy I know who has several cars that would fit the bill. All the vin numbers are removed and he can supply fake registration and insurance cards on demand, as well as license plates. You just need to be real sure your friend driving that car doesn't break any laws that would get him pulled over. Any smart cop would quickly start to smell something fishy, if you know what I mean."

"No problem there," said Pretty Boy. "The driver is a smart guy, and he's been instructed about obeying all the traffic laws. He knows the consequence of getting pulled over."

"Great, I'll get right on it, and look forward to seeing your guys tomorrow morning . . . and especially

I'll look forward to seeing that envelope!" Trigger replied as he ended the call.

•••

"Mrs. Cavanaugh, that comes to $14.60," Fatso said as he placed the last item in the grocery bag. "Those snacks look good. I'm sure you and your daughter will enjoy them."

"Oh, I'm sure we will, Fatso. We'll sit around watching all those legal programs on tv...I especially like Judge Judy, and talk about all the latest gossip while we enjoy the snacks." Mrs. Cavanaugh handed Fatso a twenty dollar bill.

Fatso counted back $5.40 change and said, "Mrs. Cavanaugh, you and your daughter have a really good visit. One last thing, do you know why Elephants need trunks?"

Mrs. Cavanaugh thought for a moment and said, "I really don't!"

"Because they don't have glove compartments!" replied Fatso with a laugh.

Mrs. Cavanaugh got a puzzled look on her face, then grinned and nodded to Fatso, grabbed her groceries, and left.

• • •

THE NEXT MORNING, 10:30 am

"Hey boss, that big semi you're looking for just pulled into our parking lot. It's taking at least half of our parking space," Fatso said over the intercom to Trigger.

"Welcome, welcome, welcome!" replied Trigger. "You just send him and his envelope back here to see me when he gets in the store."

"Will do, boss," replied Fatso as he watched the passenger side door on the truck cab open. Two guys got out and waited until the driver joined them. The three stood beside the truck talking for a couple of minutes, and then one of them started walking toward the store.

Upon entering, Fatso shouted "Hey man, what can I do for you?"

Colonel Lee walked over to the check-out counter and said to Fatso, "I think you're expecting me. I would like to talk with Mr. Green."

Fatso noticed that he was carrying an envelope, and then said, "That can be arranged. But first could you tell me where you find elephants?"

Colonel Lee just stared at Fatso.

"It all depends on where you lost 'em," Fatso said with a laugh.

Colonel Lee continued his stare

"Some guys just don't have a sense of humor," Fatso said. He then pressed a button below the counter that opened the lock going into Trigger's office in the back of the store. He then pointed toward the door and said, "Okay, buddy, Mr. Green is waiting for you in his office over there."

Colonel Lee started walking toward the office.

Upon hearing a knock on his door Trigger stood at his desk and shouted, "Come in, come in."

The two shook hands, took their seats, and Trigger said, "My name is Trigger Green, and I've been expecting you. Mr. Maggard called me yesterday to explain that you needed a car. It is parked in front of the store. I think you have an envelope there for me, and I'll exchange this one that I have that contains the car's registration and insurance information for the one you have."

The two exchanged envelopes. Colonel Lee opened his and carefully examined the documents. Trigger opened his and carefully counted the money. It was all there. A large smile then formed on his face and he said, "Everything seems to be in order. As you'll notice from your papers, the car is registered to a Mr. John Calahan. If you do get pulled over by the police, just show them the papers and tell them that Mr. Calahan is a friend of yours and let you borrow his car. That might work, and it might not. It'll be far better not to get pulled over. I'm sure Mr. Maggard explained to you the need to be careful and obey all the laws."

"He did," replied Colonel Lee. "And what about the key?"

"It's in the car . . . and the car is not locked," Trigger responded. He then stood and walked around to the door and opened it. "I wish you luck, and give my regards to Mr. Maggard when you next see him."

Colonel Lee carefully placed the envelope in his back pocket and said, "Thank you for your assistance. I will give Mr. Maggard your regards." He walked through the office door and back through the store headed for the entrance door.

Fatso shouted to him, "You have a good day! You know what you do when an elephant sneezes?"

Colonel Lee started to open the door, without comment.

"You get out of the way," said Fatso with a big smile.

Fatso watched as the man approached the other two still standing beside the truck. They talked briefly, and the man pointed toward the car parked at the far end of the lot. The three then slapped each other on the shoulders, and the fellow that came into the store went to the car, got inside, started it, and drove over in front of the truck. The car then pulled onto the highway headed in the direction of Harlan. The semi followed right behind it.

Trigger walked up beside Fatso and said, "We sure get some strange customers here! That guy looked a lot like some that have been here before. And the others were sure up to no good. Just supplying them a car shouldn't cause us any problem, but I'm going to keep my eyes and ears open to what's going on in Harlan County."

• • •

Colonel Lee looked in his rear view mirror. The truck was right behind him....he hoped it wasn't following too closely. The two vehicles had just come down a hill. He looked ahead and saw a traffic light. He checked his directions on the sheet lying on the passenger seat. This was where he would pick up route 421. He was to turn left at the traffic light. It was red when he arrived at it, so he and the truck behind waited until it turned green, and then turned left. They then followed 421 across a large mountain, called Pine Mountain. It was about 5 miles going up the mountain, and the road was very steep and curvy. They got behind several trucks that were going extremely slow, and they just followed them. It took about 20 minutes to get to the top of the mountain, and then the trucks in front picked up speed going down. But the road was still very curvy, so Colonel Lee kept his speed to no more than about 35 miles per hour. When they reached the bottom there was a fork in the road and they turned right onto a new route, 221. Colonel Lee carefully followed his directions, and after about 5 miles he saw the mail box on his right that had a big red bow tied around its post and the name 'Stepp' printed on the side of the box. He turned there onto a narrow dirt road. The semi behind him followed closely. They drove for about another half mile before coming to a clearing with the farm house and barn. Colonel Lee parked directly in front of the house. The truck pulled up to the barn. The three got out of their vehicles and met on the porch of the home.

They slapped each other on their backs and exchanged congratulations for making the journey safely. They walked through the unlocked door into the home. There was a note lying on a table just inside the door that contained instructions about how to operate everything. The note was signed by a Mr. Stepp, and concluded by wishing them a good visit and to please turn everything off and lock the door when they left.

The three went back to the truck, retrieved their suitcases, went back in the house and got all settled in. Mr. Stepp had been instructed to leave the kitchen fully stocked, and had been paid extra to cover it. They had plenty of food. Their mission was going well. They'd get started with all their activities in the morning. It had been a stressful day, and they were tired. They would just sit around and talk for a while, and then get a good night's rest.

Just then there was a loud pounding on the door. Colonel Yie was sitting nearest the door, so he jumped up, ran and opened it. Before him stood two men. They were dressed in bib overalls, large straw hats, boots, and were standing side by side. The one on the right said, "Howdy neighbors, my name's Billy Bob Johnson." He looked at the guy beside him and said, "and this here's my brother, Bubba. We lives a couple of miles from here over in that direction." He pointed behind him. "We lives with our maw, our paw's done passed. Old Mr. Stepp told us you'd be visiting here for a couple of weeks, and we just wanted to be neighborly and introduce ourselves. Be happy to help you with anything."

Bubba nodded, but didn't say anything.

Yie just looked at them, then nodded slowly, and said, "We thank you. But we're okay. We don't need anything. If you don't mind, we're tired. We just arrived. But thanks."

Bubba then spoke up, "Well, shucks, what are neighbors for. We mean to help any way we can. We'll leave you alone, but be back to check on you. You get rested up, you hear?"

With that the two brothers turned and started walking off. They walked back into the woods in the direction they had pointed.

Yie shut the door, looked at his two fellow soldiers, and said, "I'm sure that's not the last we'll see of those two. They could be trouble. We'll have to use our cover story that Mr. Maggard told us if they come back. We can't do anything to them....their mother would miss them and likely call the police. We'll just hope that we've seen the last of them, but something tells me we have not."

During their time in Knoxville with Mr. Maggard he told them if they had anyone come to the farm and saw their helicopter and other stuff to just say they worked for a private international group that flew helicopters over forest land to assess it for possible future logging activity. And that they could not discuss anything more, their work was very confidential. That's the story they would use if the Johnson brothers or anyone else inquired.

After cooking and eating their evening meal the pilots retired for the day. Starting tomorrow they had a lot to accomplish.

CHAPTER 9
KNOXVILLE, TENNESSEE

Bandit and I had truly enjoyed the past few days. We had explored around mom's property, and terrorized many squirrels and birds. But it was just fun....we hadn't really hurt any of them. I think mom has concluded that she's going to have a coon for a pet for the foreseeable future. I know that when Rosie and I have to leave we can't take Bandit with us. As nice as Sheriff Sterling is, he'd for sure draw the line at having a coon in his office! And I understand that, and hope that we can come back here for other vacations and I'll get to see and play with Bandit again.

It was about 2 o'clock in the morning, and Bandit and I were sleeping in the garage. And that's another nice thing about Bandit. Raccoons are nocturnal, and normally sleep during the day and prowl at night. But since we became friends, Bandit has adjusted his (I learned he is a boy!) sleeping pattern, and now does most of his sleeping at night, although he does, like myself, take a lot of day naps. So anyway, as I was saying, it was around 2 am when I first heard the noise. I was on my shelf, and Bandit was sleeping in my bed on the floor. I saw his head rise up, so I knew he heard the noise as well. It was coming from the garage door. The crack under the door started getting larger.....the door was opening!! My hair started to rise....I was scared. Bandit rose up and sat on his hind feet, looking straight at the garage door. It kept coming up, and after getting about half way I could see the outline of a man ducking down and entering the garage. He was wearing all dark clothes, including some kind of black headgear. He looked spooky. He was carrying a large cloth bag in his left hand, and he entered the garage very, very slowly, and was looking all around. It was still pretty dark in here, and I knew that Bandit and I could see a whole lot better than he could. He continued into the garage beside mom's car, headed toward the door into the kitchen. When he got about half way he saw Bandit sitting up looking straight at him. That's when he reached with his right hand into his pocket and pulled out a gun. He pointed it at Bandit and I heard a 'poof' sound and then Bandit fell over. He had shot Bandit, but his gun didn't make the usual loud noise. But a gun it was, and I sprang to action. He was almost to the door going into the kitchen when I jumped from my shelf. I missed his head, but landed on his outstretched right arm, the one holding the gun. My claws dug in real deep. He immediately dropped the gun, let out a scream, shook me off his right hand, and then turned and started running back out of the garage. A few seconds later I heard running in the house and then the door to the kitchen opened and Rosie and her mom came running out. Rosie had her can of mace stuck out in front of her. She turned on the light in the garage, looked down and saw me looking up at the two of them, and then she saw Bandit lying in his bed.

Rosie quickly walked over to Bandit and looked at him. "Mom, Bandit's been shot. He's bleeding!"

Mom replied, "Shot? I didn't hear any shot. Are you sure?"

"It looks like a gunshot wound to me," Rosie replied. "We've got to get him to a vet. He's breathing, and his eyes are open, but he's not moving otherwise."

"There's a 24 hour pet hospital just about a mile from here . . . I'll carry him to your car. Go get your keys and purse," mom said.

"Will do," Rosie said and trotted back toward the kitchen door. That was when she saw the gun lying on the floor. She picked it up, looked at it, and said, "It's not a real gun, it's a pellet gun. It still can do a lot of damage, but doesn't make much noise. That's why we didn't hear a gun shot."

Mom said, "Hurry, get your keys and purse. I'll have Bandit in your car." Mom picked Bandit up with the blanket he was sleeping on and carefully wrapped the blanket all around him and then carried him out to Rosie's car parked in the driveway.

Rosie came running back into the garage, looked down at me and said, "Preacher Puss you stay here in the garage. We're taking your buddy to the vet....we'll be back before too long. You guard the house."

I really wanted to go with them, but knew that I'd just be in the way, so i meowed approvingly and sat down. Rosie closed the garage door and was gone. I said a little prayer for Bandit....I sure hoped he'd be okay.

●●●

There was no traffic on the road at this hour of the morning. Rosie and mom arrived at the animal hospital in about 5 minutes and rushed Bandit inside. Rosie told the receptionist that the raccoon had been shot and she wanted the vet to look at him immediately. At first the receptionist said they didn't treat wild animals, but then, after looking at Bandit's face sticking out of the blanket said they might make an exception. She pressed the intercom button and asked the vet to please come out front. He did, and then we all went back to the operating room.

The vet said, "Ladies, we don't see many coons here at the hospital. Usually just see 'em dead on the road. Is this a special one?"

Mom replied, "He's very special, and he's my pet." She then quickly told the vet the Bandit and Preacher Puss story.

"Now that is a remarkable story if ever I heard one," the vet said as he carefully examined the wound.

He then gave Bandit a shot to put him asleep, and as he reached for his surgical tools he said, "Fortunately, it doesn't look too serious. The pellet hit him in his left shoulder, but it's still in there. It didn't pass through, so I'll have to remove it."

Both ladies looked relieved. Rosie then said, "Thank the Lord! Please proceed doctor and mom and I will get out of your way and go to the waiting room."

"Thank you ladies, it shouldn't be long," the vet replied.

After about a half hour the vet came out into the waiting room. He had a smile on his face and was carrying Bandit in a little cardboard carrier. He sat it on the counter and said, "I got the pellet out cleanly and got the wound all sanitized. Bandit won't be using that front left paw for a while, but it should heal nicely. I'm giving you some medicine to give him, and with your loving care I'm sure he'll be back good as new in a week or so. He's one lucky coon to have you ladies to care for him."

"Well, he's really good friends with my cat," Rosie said. "And he's mom's new pet. We really thank you so much for all your help."

The vet smiled and said, "It's my job. Glad to be of assistance. Now you all go back home and try and get some rest."

"Thanks again, doctor, we sure will," Rosie replied. She paid the receptionist and the threesome headed home.

CHAPTER 10
HARLAN COUNTY, KENTUCKY

Colonels Lee, Gim, and Yie were up early the next morning. They were eager to get their mission underway. After breakfast, Colonel Lee drove the rental car down the driveway to the road and parked and locked it there to block anyone else from entering their driveway. He then walked back to the farmhouse and joined his two compatriots. The three walked to the barn and opened its door. Before them was the rear of the semi containing the helicopter.

Pretty Boy Maggard had been instructed by Kim Jong-un to make certain that the farm he selected had a fork-lift capable of lifting the helicopter from the semi. After making this request of Mr. Stepp, and assuring him a bonus of $1,000 for arranging for a suitable fork-lift, Mr. Stepp had made arrangements with a friend he knew who lived near the town of Cumberland and had a fork-lift for moving bales of hay. He paid him $500 to deliver it to his farm for a two week rental. This had been done.

After opening the rear doors of the semi truck Colonel Yie said, "Colonel Gim, would you please go around to the back of the barn and get the fork-lift? Colonel Lee and I will be moving the explosives and getting the helicopter pallet ready to be moved."

"Sure thing," replied Colonel Gim as he started around the barn.

Colonels Lee and Yie then carefully removed the bomb packages and placed them in an unused stall. They then removed the fore and aft wooden braces from the pallet.

Colonel Gim rounded the corner of the barn driving the fork-lift. He parked it just outside the entrance door, jumped off, and joined the other two.

"Okay Gim," said Colonel Gim, "Everything is all set to remove the helicopter. Be very careful getting the fork-lift blades into the pallet, and then lift and place the helicopter anywhere in front of the barn that doesn't have any power cables around."

"I can do that," Colonel Gim replied.

He jumped back on the fork-lift and then carefully drove it into position at the back of the semi. He slowly raised the forks up to the correct height to go into the pallet upon which the helicopter rested, and then very slowly moved the forks into the pallet. He gently raised the pallet off the semi truck bed just a couple of inches, and slowly reversed the fork-lift out of the barn.

"My lord, Bubba, what in the world is that thing they're moving out of the barn?" Billy Bob Johnson said to his brother. The two had walked to the Stepp farm from their home to again offer to be of assistance to the Stepp tenants, but just as they got to the clearing where the woods stopped at the Stepp farm they saw the tenants moving something from the barn with a fork-lift. They decided to just observe for a bit before announcing their presence.

"Durnest thing I ever saw," replied Bubba. "It kinda looks like one them hell-e-copter things to me."

"It does," said Billy Bob. "And that's a mighty rare sight around these parts."

"It is," replied Bubba. "What you reckon they gonna do with it?"

"Fly it, I guess," said Billy Bob. "But I shore don't know what fer!"

The brothers then proceeded walking toward the barn.

"Careful, careful," said Colonel Yie to Colonel Gim as the later was touching down with the pallet and helicopter. He had found a nice level spot without any overhead lines about 50 feet in front of the garage and had just lowered the pallet to the ground there. Colonels Yie and Lee stood beside the fork-lift.

"Well I'll be dog-gonned," Bubba said loudly as he and brother Billy Bob arrived on the other side of the fork-lift. "That there's sure some hell-e-copter."

All three colonels jerked their heads toward the voice. By reflex, Colonels Yie and Lee dropped their right hands to their side trying to locate their sidearms..... but they were not there. They then all three recognized the two men standing now beside them.

Billy Bob said, "Mornin neighbors. Ole Bubba here and me, we just thought we should come back over this morning to see if you had a good night, and to see if you might need help with anything. We aim to be neighborly and helpful."

Colonel Lee then spoke, "Good morning Johnsons. We did have a good evening, and now are starting our work. This is indeed a helicopter. The three of us work for an international company that purchases timber rights. We fly this helicopter to look at the trees and assess their value. If we find land with trees of sufficient quality, we then negotiate with the land owners for the timber rights. Our parent company then makes arrangements for logging to begin on the property. Everything we do is very confidential, so we would greatly appreciate your not letting anyone know what we're doing. Would you do that for us?"

Billy Bob put a finger up to his lips and said, "No one will hear a thing from us, ain't that right Bubba?"

"Right as rain," Bubba replied. "We ain't gonna say nothing bout it. But we sure would like to go for a ride in that fancy hell-e-copter you got there."

The Colonels looked at each other and Colonel Lee grinned and said, "We'll try and arrange that a little later. We were just now getting everything unloaded and set-up."

"No big rush at all," said Bubba. "Ole Billy Bob here and me, we never laid eyes on anything like that before. Not too many of those come to Harlan County."

"I understand," Colonel Lee replied.

"Where you boys from," asked Billy Bob

The three colonels again looked at each other, and then Colonel Lee said, "As I stated, we're from an international company that's headquartered in China. But don't forget that that's our little secret."

"Oh, we ain't forgettin," replied Billy Bob. "Mum's the word. We was just curious. And before I forget it, Maw wanted to invite you all to supper with us tomorrow night. We eats about 6. We're the first driveway on your left as you leave Mr. Stepp's farm. Just a couple of miles down the road. Our names there on the mailbox....you can't miss it. Maw fixes real good vitals, so you needs to come real hungry."

Again the three colonels looked at each other. Colonel Lee replied, "That's very nice of your mother. Thank you, we'll be there. Now if you don't mind we need to check out a few things here....we've lots of work to do, so please do excuse us. We'll look forward to seeing you at 6 pm tomorrow."

"Shucks, it was nothing," Bubba said. "If there ain't nothing else we can do fer you we'll be heading out. And don't forget about that ride in the hell-e-copter."

"Oh we won't forget," Colonel Lee said. "You two have a good day, and we'll see you tomorrow."

"Good," Billy Bob said. Bubba and Billy Bob then shook hands with each of the colonels and then started their walk home. After getting out of hearing range Bubba said, "Billy Bob, we got us some real strange neighbors. Three Chi-nee-men and a hell-e-copter. Real strange."

"Real strange," replied Billy Bob

After driving the fork-lift back into the barn, Colonel Gim stood with his two fellow soldiers in front of the barn beside the helicopter. Colonel Yie said,

"Gentlemen, those two are definitely a problem. We really can't afford to let anything happen to them that would bring attention to us, so I think it was a very good idea to go along with offering them a helicopter ride and agreeing to have a meal with them. We can avoid the ride by delaying it until we've finished our mission, but we'll have to go to the meal tomorrow night. So let's get on with our tasks."

The soldiers then started to ready the helicopter. The Robinson R22 Beta II is a two place, light utility vehicle with a maximum speed of approximately 115 miles per hour. It is powered by a Lycoming O-360 four-cylinder engine. It has a two bladed rotor system that permits easy transporting. It has an empty weight of only 865 pounds, and can accommodate two persons with baggage weighing a total of not more than 400 pounds, plus 16.9 gallons of fuel weighing 101 pounds. It is approximately 28 feet long, 9 feet tall, and 6.3 feet wide. It is operated by a pistol grip, center-positioned cyclic.

Colonel Lee climbed aboard the helicopter and started it. He then lifted off the pallet and hovered. The other two colonels grabbed the pallet and carried it back into the barn. Colonel Lee then landed the helicopter on the flat ground, turned off the engine, and climbed out.

Colonels Gim and Yie came out of the barn each carrying a 'dummy' bomb. Like the real bombs, the dummies were contained in a bag similar to a shopping bag, with straps on the top. The real bombs had detonators placed in the bottom of the bag such that when they were dropped and struck an object the detonators would trigger the C-4 explosives. The dummy bombs simply had bricks in them to simulate the weight of the explosives. One dummy bomb was attached to the front of each helicopter skid by dropping the loop in the attachment rope over the front end of the skid and then securely tying the other end to the straps on the top of the bomb bag. The metal box in the middle of the rope contained the actuator that, when activated by the remote control, would release the rope below that was attached to the bomb. Both dummy bombs were securely attached to the skids.

Colonel Lee then proclaimed, "Okay, it looks like we're ready for our first flight and test. Colonel Yie will serve as the navigator and bombardier, and I will pilot. Colonel Gim will maintain radio contact with us, and should we require help we'll call him. Okay?"

The other colonels nodded approval. Colonel Yie then jumped in the helicopter in the right seat with radio and remote control in hand. Colonel Lee situated himself in the left seat and grabbed the cyclic. Colonel Gim stood away from the helicopter with radio in hand and gave the crew a thumb-up signal. The craft started to rise slowly. The ropes holding the dummy bombs to the front ends of the skids were about 3 feet long and became taut and hung directly down as the aircraft lifted. It then began to pick up both vertical and forward speed, and very quickly became just a speck in the sky to Colonel Gim.

Colonel Lee flew the craft for about 5 minutes before spotting a small water pond located in a very remote area. He said to Colonel Yie, "That pond looks to be about the size of a large farm house. For our test today how about we try to drop our bombs directly in the middle of the pond?"

Colonel Yie smiled and gave a nod and a thumb-up in reply. He then grabbed the remote control for the bomb actuators and held it firmly in his left hand, with his right forefinger positioned just above the red button that, when depressed, would signal the actuators to release the dummy bombs.

Colonel Lee took the helicopter up to a height of about 5,000 feet and positioned the craft directly over the pond below. He looked at his bombardier and gave a nod. Colonel Yie pressed the red button. The front of the helicopter rotated upward as the loads were released. The crew then watched as the two dummy bombs fell through the air toward their target. One landed almost directly in the center of the pond, the other about midway between center and the pond shore. The two men looked at each other with huge smiles. They each gave the other a thumb-up, and then Colonel Lee moved the cyclic to head for home.

CHAPTER 11
HARLAN, KENTUCKY

Creech Cafe is located directly across Central Street from the Harlan County court house. Fred Knapp is the owner. He inherited the cafe from his father many years ago. It is a very popular gathering place for both the young, old, and not-so-old. Kids gather at Creech's daily after school to both have some refreshments and to discuss the day's activities and gossip about classmates. Old timers gather and sit for hours drinking coffee and cussing and discussing local, state, national, and world problems. Fred Knapp is also the mayor of Harlan. He is very popular, and enjoys greatly greeting, serving, and talking with all his customers. The cafe has two unusual features. The first is a parrot named Polly. The bird sits on a perch above the front door and greets those entering and leaving. Polly has a very good vocabulary and appetite. She frequently mooches food from customers, but is greatly loved by all who frequent the cafe. The second unusual feature of Creech's is the wall coverings. Fred has clipped interesting articles from the local newspaper, the **Harlan Daily Enterprise**, and pinned them on the walls along with hundreds of photographs and articles from other newspapers and magazines depicting various persons and events. These almost completely cover all the cafe walls. Fred loves to have customers ask about any article or photograph. He'll spend hours explaining and embellishing them. Fred also loves to tell jokes, and has tremendously enhanced the otherwise dreary day of many customers by sharing a joke with them. It is indeed a popular Harlan hangout.

Sheriff J. Bert Sterling and Deputy Kyle Potter frequently visited Creech's for coffee, to discuss town business with Mayor Knapp, and/or just to take a break from the office. Today they were having coffee at a table in the back of the cafe. Mayor Knapp had joined them, and had placed a carafe of coffee on their table.

"You do know that Preacher Puss is the talk of the town don't you Bert?" Fred asked.

"Yeah, I know," replied the sheriff. "It really shouldn't be a problem, but it seems like everyone I run into wants to talk about that cat. And it's taking a lot of my time."

Deputy Potter nodded in response, and added, "That goes for me too. Since that nice article about her adventures with Rosie in Tennessee was published in the *Enterprise* it seems everyone in Harlan County knows about her special talents."

Fred said, "You got that right." He pointed toward a recent posting on the wall behind sheriff Sterling and said, "That's the article, right there. The reporter sure did a complete story. She told everything in a lot of detail that Preacher Puss did while on vacation with Rosie. And very remarkable they are."

The sheriff replied, "Yeah, Rosie gave a detailed description of her vacation activities to the reporter. I think the interview took a little over an hour. And then the story appeared on the front page of the *Enterprise*. We've even had phone calls from citizens saying that Preacher Puss should be awarded some kind of special metal or honor for all she's done. And I really couldn't argue with that. She's a very special cat."

Fred replied, "Well, why don't we jointly come up with some kind of special recognition for her, from both the City of Harlan and from the sheriff's office? Maybe a formal certificate officially making her an honorary deputy? I think the citizens of Harlan County would greatly approve and support such an honor."

Bert and Kyle looked at each other, and then Kyle replied, "Fred, I think you've come up with yet another brilliant idea. We could get a nice certificate printed up, frame it, and then hang it beside her shelf in the office. It would be noticed by everyone that entered."

"Good idea," said Fred. "But in addition I think we should have a big ceremony presenting it to her, and invite the press to cover it. Heck, it could be carried state wide . . . maybe even nationally."

The sheriff, after reflecting for a bit, said, "You know, I like the idea. And something else that I bet would work would be to have the presentation at the Slusher Brothers' farm. After all, Preacher Puss really was their cat before coming to the sheriff's office. And ole Gunsmoke and Booger just love her to death, and I know that Preacher Puss would enjoy visiting with them and their cats. The great room at their farm house would accommodate a lot of people for the presentation. What'd you think about having it there?"

Fred pounded his fist down on the table, sloshing some coffee from the cups, and said, "Boys, we've just come up with a super idea. I just love to get publicity for Harlan, being the mayor and all, and I know that the idea would go over well. When can we set it up?"

Kyle replied, "I think the sooner the better. Strike while the iron's hot, as the old saying goes. The recent *Enterprise* article has really focused attention on

Preacher Puss, so her getting this special recognition would certainly be in order."

"I'll call the Slusher Brothers and see when they might let us do it," Bert said. "Just as soon as I know, I'll let you know and we'll also alert the *Enterprise* so they can publicize it. That be okay?"

Fred and Kyle both nodded their approval. After finishing their coffee the three stood and slowly started walking toward the door. As they passed a recent wall posting Fred pointed to it and said, "Did you fellows see that one in the *Knoxville News-Sentinel*?"

Both Bert and Kyle shook their heads negatively, and Bert said, "No, but I'll bet you're getting ready to tell us all about it!"

Fred got a big smile on his face, took a deep breath, and started, "Well, the story goes something like this. That picture you see right there shows an overturned hay wagon. This farmer in East Tennessee was trying to move a huge load of hay on his wagon driven by a couple of horses. Apparently one of the wagon wheels slipped off the road and caused the wagon to turn over, spilling all the hay. One of the guys neighbors came along and offered to help clean up the spill, but told the wagon driver that his wife had lunch ready and invited the driver to lunch with him, and then they would come back out and clean up the spill. The wagon driver said, "I don't know, Pa ain't gonna like it."

The neighbor said, "Oh your Pa won't care if you have lunch before we clean up the hay. You need a little rest before we start anyway."

"Well," the wagon driver said, " I guess that'd be okay, but I still think Pa ain't gonna like it."

The two went to the neighbors home and had a good and leisurely lunch, after which they sat in rocking chairs on the neighbors front porch. After doing the chit-chat for about 30 minutes the neighbor said, "Well, I guess we should get back and clean up that hay."

The wagon driver said, "Yeah, we should, but I'm sure Pa ain't gonna like it."

The neighbor then said, "Say, where is your Pa anyway?"

The wagon driver said, "He's under the wagon!"

The threesome then roared with laughter. Bert slapped Fred on the back and said, "Fred, that's a great story. And I'll bet for sure that Pa didn't like it!

As Bert and Kyle went out the front door each reached up and petted Polly, who was sitting on her perch.

Polly said, "Come back boys. Come back boys."

•••

I heard the door open and saw Bert and Kyle walk into the office. They each turned around and gave me a good pet. I sat up, gently wagged my tail, and gave an approving meow. I watched as they walked to the counter behind which Rosie sat.

Rosie looked up and said, "Hey guys, get your fill of coffee from Fred?"

"We did," Bert replied. "And while we were having coffee we came up with a plan to give recognition to Preacher Puss for all her heroics."

"I'm all ears," Rosie replied.

And my ears perked up as well. I couldn't wait to hear about this!

Bert and Kyle then proceeded to tell Rosie about the plans to make me a deputy with a framed certificate and ceremony at the Slusher Brother's farm, with the press invited.

"That's just a really wonderful idea," Rosie said. "And I bet I can come up with a cute little deputy's uniform that Preacher Puss can wear."

The three of them then looked over at me. I was truly excited, and loved what they said they were going to do for me, although a tad reserved about wearing any kind of uniform. Well, anyway, it will likely work out fine, so I gave three loud meow's and several tail swishes in approval.

Sheriff Sterling then said, "That sounded like approval from Preacher Puss. I'll go call the Slushers to see if they agree to host the ceremony." Bert then walked into his office closing the door behind him.

I laid back down on my blanketed shelf and closed my eyes for a very contented nap. My last thought before dozing off was that I was going to be famous!

•••

"Hey Gunsmoke, how's everything at the Slusher farm?" Bert asked using his private cell phone.

"Real good," replied Gunsmoke. "George, Charlie, Ray, and all my good North Korean friends are hard at work, and all my cats are doing well. And Booger seems happy as a lark....so, yeah, I guess everything is good. To what do I owe the pleasure of this phone call from Harlan County's finest?"

The sheriff replied, "I know you're aware of all the publicity that ole Preacher Puss has been getting lately, and while having coffee this morning with Fred and

Kyle at Creech's we happened upon an idea that I think you'll like."

"Lay it on me," Gunsmoke replied.

Bert proceeded to relate to Gunsmoke the idea of making Preacher Puss a deputy by having a ceremony at the Slusher farm and inviting the media to attend.

"Best darn idea I ever did hear," replied Gunsmoke. "You knew we'd go along with it, but I appreciate your asking. That cat is something truly special, and she deserves all the recognition she can get. When were you thinking about having the ceremony?"

Bert said, "At your convenience. But we would need a little time to inform the media and let them arrange to be there. So, today is Wednesday. How about if we try to set it up for next Wednesday...would that work with you?

"Finer than frog hair," Gunsmoke said. "We'll be all set up here in our great room to accommodate a lot of folks. And we'll have some refreshments for everyone. You just tell them to identify themselves to Charlie at the gate on their way in. Could you supply me with a list of names that I could give to Charlie. We do have to be real careful who we let in . . . there's so many nuts around these days."

The sheriff said, "Oh, believe me, I do understand that. Sure, that'll be no problem. I'll have Rosie keep track of everyone and get the list to you at least by next Tuesday. Will that be okay?"

"Absolutely," replied Gunsmoke. "I just can't wait! It'll be so good seeing ole Preacher Puss and everyone. I'll also try to round up as many of our cats as I can and have them in the house to play with Preacher Puss. I think she'll enjoy that."

"Without doubt," Bert replied. "I can't thank you enough. I really appreciate your cooperation and support."

"No problem. Glad to be of service. You take care now, you hear?" Gunsmoke said.

"You bet. You too, Gunsmoke. See you next Wednesday if not before," Bert replied as he ended the phone call.

He then walked back into the front office and related the plans to Rosie.

"Oh, goodie! I'm going to call Mrs. Cavanaugh right now to see if she can make Preacher Puss a deputy's outfit. It will be so cute!!" Rosie said.

Bert's voice had awakened me from my nap, and I heard the conversation he had with Rosie about my upcoming ceremony. Next Wednesday was going to be a day I'll long remember. But I still have some reservations about wearing that uniform. After all, what will all the other cats at the Slusher farm think about me wearing a uniform? They might make fun of me. But I guess if it pleases Rosie and the sheriff I'll just have to put up with it.

• • •

"Why hello Rosie, how in the world are you?" asked Mrs. Cavanaugh as she answered Rosie's phone call. Mrs. Cavanaugh lived only a short walking distance from Maggard's Grocery, and was a frequent customer there. She was a widow, and supplemented her social security income by sewing. She was an expert seamstress, and had recently made a beautiful Santa Claus uniform for Fatso to wear to a Christmas party.

"I'm doing real good, Mrs. Cavanaugh," replied Rosie. "I was calling because I have a very special request for you."

Mrs. Cavanaugh said, "Oh my, that sounds exciting. Please tell me what it is."

Rosie said, "I know you are well aware of Preacher Puss, the famous cat that lives here in the sheriff's office."

"Oh, everyone in Harlan County knows about that cat," replied Mrs. Cavanaugh.

"Well, the Mayor and the sheriff have decided to have a real special ceremony at the Slusher brother's farm one week from today to honor Preacher Puss and make her a deputy. Lots of media will be there, and it will get a lot of attention. It was my idea to ask if you would be willing to make a uniform for Preacher Puss. Her picture will appear in a lot of newspapers and magazines, and I thought if she was wearing a cute little deputy's uniform it would just add a lot. What do you think?"

Mrs. Cavanaugh replied, "I must say, I've never been asked to sew a uniform for a cat! I suppose I could do it. It certainly wouldn't require much material, but it'd need to be the same material as the other deputy's uniforms. But, yes, yes, I think I could do it. You would need to bring the cat here for me to make measurements, and maybe you could bring an extra deputy's uniform that I could cut up for the material. Could you do that?"

"No problem whatsoever," replied Rosie. "I want you to have as much time as possible to make it, so how about if I bring Preacher Puss to your house tomorrow morning, maybe around 10 am? And we do have a lot of extra uniforms, so I'll bring one of those as well."

"Perfect," Mrs. Cavanaugh said. "See you tomorrow at 10."

CHAPTER 12
HARLAN COUNTY, KENTUCKY

The Colonels had just finished their breakfast, and were still seated at the dining table talking.

Colonel Lee said, "Yesterday's test flight went well. The Robinson chopper flew easily, and the trial bomb drop was almost exactly on target. I think we can all now feel confident with that part of our mission. We now must concentrate on a more difficult phase, that of finding a way to make certain that all the traitors are in the Slusher farm house when we bomb it. As you know, our Supreme Leader will not accept anything short of total success. If even one of the traitors is still alive after our bomb drop Kim will consider the mission a failure and we will pay the ultimate price when we return home. So we must determine a suitable day and time when all the traitors will be in the home."

Colonel Lee then pulled a piece of paper from his notebook and studied it. On it were the names of the ex-North Korean soldiers that were now at the Slusher farm.

The names were:

General O Kuk-mu

General Park Chang-sun

General Sin Ji-hae

Bin Yo-han

Choe Yong-ho

Seo Chi-won

Ryu Jae-gyu

"Seven deserters," said Colonel Lee. "These seven have disgraced our country and our Supreme Leader and must all be eliminated."

Colonels Yie and Gim nodded in agreement.

Colonel Lee continued, "We simply must find a day and time when all seven will for sure be in the Slusher farm house. It would be a lot simpler if we could fly the Robinson at night, when all of them would be asleep, but, unfortunately, the mission could be greatly compromised if not flown during daylight hours. The darkness would present too much of a challenge for us to fly to the target and then successfully drop the bombs. We must find a time during daylight hours when we know for sure all seven will be present."

"What is the plan to find such a time?" asked Colonel Gim.

Colonel Lee replied, "Mr. Maggard provided us with a contact in Mr. Green, where we got our automobile as we arrived. I am going to drive back to Maggard's Grocery this morning and have a discussion with Mr. Green to see if he can give us the name of someone in the town of Harlan that I could contact. This person would have to be very knowledgeable of all the happenings in the county and would also need to be of low intelligence and willing to cooperate with us for money. Mr. Maggard had asked Mr. Green to please cooperate with us, and I will offer Mr. Green $2500 for the information."

"That sounds good," replied Colonel Yie. "I hope Mr. Green will know of such a person."

"So while I'm gone to see Mr. Green, the two of you could be getting everything ready for more test flights starting tomorrow. We must familiarize ourselves with the terrain between here and the Slusher farm. We will do several flights there to make certain we know all the landmarks between here and there," Colonel Lee said.

"I have a question," said Colonel Yie. "How do we identify the Slusher farm house?"

Colonel Lee responded, "Ah, an excellent question, Yie. I forgot to mention to you that after talking with Mr. Green I will ask him directions on how to get to the

Slusher farm. I will then drive there and upon arriving I will record the coordinates on my portable GPS. Then when we fly there I'll simply fly the Robinson to those coordinates."

Colonels Yie and Gim nodded in agreement.

"Now, the other matter for today is the visit for dinner with the Johnsons tonight," said Colonel Lee. "We will go, but we must be very careful not to reveal anything about our true mission. If the Johnsons thought that we were doing anything illegal they would likely contact law enforcement....and we certainly don't want that. So we just go and enjoy the food and have general discussions with them. Are you both okay with that?"

Yie and Gim nodded in agreement.

• • •

Fatso looked out the window at Maggard's Grocery. He then punched the intercom button to talk with Trigger Green and said, "Hey boss, that strange Chinaman that was here earlier with the semi and got the car from us is back. He just parked out front and is headed for the door."

"Send him back when he gets in," replied Trigger Green.

"Will do," Fatso replied.

As Colonel Lee entered Maggard's Grocery Fatso greeted him, "Welcome, welcome, welcome my friend. I'll bet you're here to see Mr. Green."

Colonel Lee replied, "Yes, I would like to see him."

"That can be arranged," Fatso replied. "But first, can you tell me which elephants don't get toothaches?"

The colonel stared at Fatso.

Fatso said, "Those that use Crest!"

The colonel continued to stare.

Fatso giggled and said, "Okay, head on back to his office. I'll press the button to unlock the door. I think he's expecting you."

Colonel Lee walked to the back of the grocery and, after gently knocking on the door, opened it and entered.

Trigger Green stood from his desk and walked around to shake hands with Colonel Lee. He said, "It is a pleasure to see you again. I hope the car is running fine."

"Oh yes, the car is good," replied the colonel. "I've come on another matter. Mr. Maggard said if I needed any assistance to contact you."

"Always be happy to help when I can," Trigger replied. "Exactly what did you have in mind?"

Colonel Lee began, "I really have two needs, and I have $2500 in this envelope for your help."

Trigger's eyes lit up as he took the envelope and said, "Be delighted to be of assistance!"

The colonel continued, "My first need is to find someone in the town of Harlan that knows generally what is going on in Harlan County, is not particularly bright, and who will pass along information to me for money. Of course I would expect him to keep all the information strictly confidential. The second need is to be given the directions to the Slusher Brothers farm. I need to contact them on a matter."

Trigger thought about these requests, and then said, "I think I know just the person that would fullfill your first need. And I'll be happy to have Fatso draw you a map with directions to the Slusher Brother's farm. No problem. But I would like to ask why you need to go there?"

Colonel Lee said, "It is a confidential matter. I just need to personally deliver a note to them."

"Okay," Trigger said. "But when you drive there you'll encounter a gate to the farm and there will be a guard named Charlie at the gate. He won't let you in unless you have an appointment."

Richard G. Edwards

"No problem," the colonel said. "I can just give my note to him and ask that he deliver it personally to one of the Slusher brothers."

Trigger thought again for a moment and then said, "Okay, it's a deal. The person in Harlan that fits your requirements is named Bennie Sekao. Bennie is the town drunk. He's certainly not the brightest of persons, but when he's sober he's reliable and knows generally most of the things going on in the county. He's always interested in earning some money, which will promptly be spent for alcohol. You can usually find Bennie sitting on the wall that surrounds the Harlan County Court House. I'll have Fatso write down his name and description. I don't think you'll have any trouble locating him. Also, Fatso will have your map and directions to the Slusher Brothers Farm. Will that take care of our deal?"

"I think that should be sufficient," the colonel replied.

Trigger pressed the intercom button and relayed the instructions to Fatso. He then stood and shook hands with the colonel and said, "Come back anytime. I'm always here and willing to be helpful to any friend of Pretty Boy Maggard."

"Thank you Mr. Green," the colonel said as he shook hands with Trigger. He then turned and walked out of the office and toward the grocery store check-out counter.

Fatso said, "Okay, I think I understand what Mr. Green wanted me to give you. First of all, here's a description of Bennie Sekao and directions to where you'll likely find him. And I just drew up this little map with directions to the Slusher Brother's farm. Take a look at it, and if you have questions I'll be happy to try and answer them."

Colonel Lee read the information on the sheet that Fatso handed him. After studying it for a couple of moments he said, "I think I understand. This should be all I need. Thank you."

"No problem," Fatso replied. But before you leave, could you tell me what looks like an elephant and flies?"

The colonel thought a moment, and then said, "No, nothing like that comes to mind."

"A flying elephant," Fatso replied with a smile.

Colonel Lee, with a puzzled look on his face, turned and left.

•••

He followed the directions to Harlan, and then to the Harlan County Court House. It was mid-morning. He parked his car on Central Street almost in front of a restaurant called Creech Cafe. He sat in his car looking toward the court house and trying to locate the man called Bennie Sekao. There were several people sitting on the low wall that surrounded the court house. Finally he spotted one fitting the description written down by Fatso. He got out of his car and walked over to where the man was sitting. He approached him and said, "Are you by chance Mr. Sekao?"

Bennie looked up at him and said, "I'm only called that by the judge. Everyone else just calls me Bennie."

Colonel Lee extended his hand and said, "I'm very pleased to make your acquaintance. My name is Mr. Lee."

Bennie shook hands and said, "I don't think I've seen you around here before. Should I know you?"

Colonel Lee responded, "No, I've never been to Harlan before. But a business acquaintance, a Mr. Trigger Green, told me that you might be interested in working for me."

"Oh, Trigger sent you! Well, yeah, I would be interested. What would you like me to do and how much will you pay me?"

Colonel Lee looked around to be sure no one was close enough to hear their conversation, and said, "I'm just interested in a little information. Mr. Green said that you knew most everything that was happening in Harlan County. I'm an attorney and represent a client that wishes me to deliver a special offer to the North Koreans living at the Slusher Brothers farm, and I need to know when I might be able to catch all seven of them together at the farm. It's vitally important that all seven be present. And it must be during daylight hours, not at night. When I have that information I will arrange to go there and present all seven of them this special offer. It's very important that it be a surprise. They must not know anything about me or my special offer until I meet them. That's about all the information I'm free to share with you. If you would like to do this work for me I'll pay you $200 now, and another $800 when you've given me the needed information. But you must agree to tell no one about our arrangement. Everything must be kept secret. What do you think?"

Bennie's eyes got real big, and he said, "Mr. Lee, we have a deal. Everything on the hush-hush. All will be secret. Now all you've got to do is give me the $200 and then tell me how we get back together after

I've learned when all seven will be at the farm during daylight hours."

Colonel Lee withdrew an envelope from his folder, handed it to Bennie, and said, "Today is Thursday. I'll give you two days to come up with the information." He then pointed toward his car and said, "That brown Chevrolet over there belongs to me. I'll come back on Saturday afternoon around 4 pm and park as close as I can to where I'm presently parked. When you spot me you come to the car. I'll have your $800 in exchange for the information. Can you do that?"

After counting the money in the envelope, Bennie shook hands with Colonel Lee and said, "No problem at all. I know I can get the information by then. I'll see you Saturday around 4 o'clock."

Colonel Lee nodded approval, turned, and walked back to his car.

•••

Again following the directions he had received from Fatso, Colonel Lee turned off highway 119 onto the road that lead to the Slusher farm. He soon arrived at the guard gate. He rolled down his window and heard the guard, wearing a nametag that said Charlie, say, "May I ask who you are and what you're doing here?"

"I'm just a lost tourist. I was looking for some place to take pictures of these beautiful mountains and trees."

"This is not that place," Charlie said. "You've come to the end of the road, and this is a private road. Please turn around and resume your search elsewhere."

"Yes, officer, I will indeed," the colonel replied. "I'm sorry to have troubled you."

"No trouble at all," said Charlie, "You have a good day."

Colonel Lee reached down to the portable GPS in the passenger seat and pressed the button to record the current location coordinates. He then spoke to Charlie saying, "Yes Officer, you have a good day as well."

After turning his car around Colonel Lee headed back to the Stepp Farm.

•••

It was 5:30 pm. The three military men had all met back at the Stepp farm house and had discussed the events of the day. Colonels Yie and Gim had done further testing and maintenance on the Robinson

Helicopter, and all had gone well. Colonel Lee told them about his trip, and all agreed that everything was proceeding on schedule. They now were getting ready to leave for dinner with the Johnsons.

After driving their car to the main road and turning left, the three military men traveled a couple miles before coming to the next mailbox on the left side of the road. It had the name 'Johnson' printed on it. They turned into the gravel driveway and drove about one half mile before coming to the house. Actually, it was not a house, but a mobile home. They pulled up to it and parked.

They looked at each other, and Colonel Lee said, "I think this is what is called a mobile home. It's manufactured at a remote location and then moved on wheels to its final resting place. I understand they are very popular here in the United States. They cost much less than a conventional home."

The three got out of their car, walked to the front door, and knocked.

The door flew open and an elderly woman stood facing them. She said, "Lordy be, you shore is Chi-nee-men. You come right on in. I been expectin you. Billy Bob and Bubba done told me all about you. I got you a real fine supper all fixed. Them boys is in bed taking a nap . . . I'll holler fer em . . . Billy Bob, Bubba, you get yourselves in here. We's got company."

"Everybody just calls me Maw....so you can too," Maw said. "You boys have a seat over there and I'll finish supper. The boys will be in directly."

"Thank you, Maw," Colonel Lee responded as they sat on the couch.

"Well if it ain't our Chi-nee-men neighbors!" Billy Bob said as he and Bubba walked into the living room.

"Hi Johnsons," Colonel Lee said. "We met your mother, and are looking forward to our meal with you."

"Oh I think you'll like it," Bubba replied. "Maw cooks real good. And tonight she's done cooked up a big pot of soup beans seasoned with hog jowl and fatback. And a big skillet of hot corn bread, and we's got real butter to put on it. Plus we got a good mess of turnip greens seasoned with Maw's special secret sauce, and then we'll top it all off with the best apple pie you ever put in your mouth. Now how's that sound to you?"

"Interesting," Colonel Lee replied.

"Shucks, it'll be a meal you won't forget. And we don't even know your names!" said Billy Bob.

Colonel Lee said, "Oh, so sorry. We should have introduced ourselves. I'm Mr. Lee, and my two associates here are Mr. Yie and Mr. Gim. Please just call us Lee, Yie, and Gim."

"Sounds like some kind of rock music group," Bubba said with a laugh. "But we be proud to make your acquaintance."

Maw called out, "Come and get it." and everyone moved to the kitchen table for the meal. Then she said, "Bow your heads boys, I'm turning thanks."

Billy Bob and Bubba bowed their heads. The three soldiers first looked at each other, and then slowly bowed their heads following the lead of the others.

Maw then said, "Lord, we give you thanks for this food which we are about to eat. We thanks you too for our Chi-nee-men guests. We know that all we have comes from you, and we thank you for all our many blessings. Amen."

Billy Bob and Bubba said in unison, "Amen."

Maw said, "Well, dig in. Don't be bashful. And feel free to crumble up cornbread into them beans.... everybody round here does it."

The colonels watched as the brothers took large pieces of cornbread and crumbled them into their bowls of beans. They then followed suit.

The six then proceeded to eat their meal and do the chit-chat, carefully avoiding any talk of their mission, and repeated several times to the Johnsons that their job in Kentucky was very confidential and they just couldn't talk about it. The Johnsons seemed to understand and continued to make small talk.

After the apple pie Colonel Lee said, "Johnsons, this has been a very delightful evening. Exceptional food, and delightful company. I know I speak for my two associates when I sincerely thank you for inviting us. We will long remember your hospitality."

Maw replied, "Shucks, it was nothing. We enjoyed it too."

Bubba said, "We did, and me and Billy Bob are shore looking forward to our rides in your hell-e-copter, ain't we Billy Bob?"

"For shore," Billy Bob replied.

"We'll be working on getting that arranged for you. It may be several days before we can work it into our schedules, but we won't forget. And thanks again for the great evening," Colonel Lee said as the three turned to leave.

"You come back anytime," Maw said.

After getting in their car and starting the drive home Colonel Gim said, "One thing for sure, that was an evening we'll never forget! The food was delicious, but I'm really not too sure what we ate. I guess it was what they call traditional Kentucky food."

Colonel Yie replied, "I agree. I think I had previously eaten apple pie a few times, but never had I eaten any of the other food. And it was indeed tasty!"

It had been a long day. As soon as the three soldiers got back to the Stepp farm they retired for the evening.

CHAPTER 13
HARLAN COUNTY, KENTUCKY

Earlier that same day, Thursday

Mrs. Cavanaugh lives alone, her husband having passed away many years ago. She has a modest home within walking distance of Maggard's Grocery, where she frequently does her shopping. She is a very accomplished seamstress, and many people in the county hire her to sew something special. She has two pets, one is a goldfish named Goldie. The other is a cat named Sylvester. She had her cat for about two years prior to getting the goldfish. Before getting Goldie, Sylvester, a mixed breed black and white male, spent about half his time inside and the other half outside Mrs. Cavanaugh's home. When she got the goldfish she quickly learned that the two pets could not coexist. After two episodes of catching Sylvester with a paw in the goldfish bowl, Mrs. Cavanaugh banned him to the outside. She only allows him in for brief visits when she can keep an eye on both the cat and the goldfish.

She loves them both. She was looking forward this morning to Rosie Cain's visit. Rosie would be bringing Preacher Puss for Mrs. Cavanaugh to measure for her uniform. Mrs. Cavanaugh had gone to Maggard's Grocery earlier and picked up some snacks for Rosie's visit. She also bought a package of Whisker Lickins cat treats. She knew from articles published in the **Harlan Daily Enterprise** that Preacher Puss really liked them so she planned to give both Preacher Puss and Sylvester a few of the special treats. She had allowed her cat to come into the house, and she was sitting in her living room keeping an eye on him and the goldfish while waiting for Rosie and Preacher Puss to arrive. Sylvester had promptly located himself on a shelf close to the fish bowl and was staring at Goldie as the fish swam around in the bowl. His tail was swishing broad strokes with an occasional quiver. His eyes followed every movement of the fish. He really wanted to pounce on Goldie, but feared the consequences from Mrs. Cavanaugh if he did. Mrs. Cavanaugh had a nice smile on her face as she gently rocked back and forth in her rocker.

Sylvester saw them first. He jerked his head to look through the front window as movement outside caught his attention. Mrs. Cavanaugh said, "It's okay Sylvester, it's just Rosie and Preacher Puss arriving for their appointment. Now I want you to behave and be a good cat. You leave Goldie alone and you play good with Preacher Puss. I even have some treats for you cats."

I was greatly enjoying this outing. Rosie had arranged for her sister Posey to fill in for her while she was gone from the sheriff's office, and she had placed me in my cat-carrier and the two of us had driven from Harlan to Mrs. Cavanaugh's home. I had enjoyed looking at everything along the way. Rosie usually let me move freely in the car, but today she said it would be a lot more convenient for me to travel in the cat-carrier. But she propped it up on a pillow in the car's passenger seat so that I might be able to see out. It was a treat for me.

We arrived, and Rosie carried me to the door of Mrs. Cavanaugh's home and knocked.

Mrs. Cavanaugh opened the door and said, "Welcome, welcome. Rosie and Preacher Puss. It's so good to see you both. Please do come in."

Just as soon as we entered her living room I spotted Sylvester. This was my first time to visit here and I had not known she had a cat. Sylvester was looking directly at me as Rosie placed the carrier on the floor and opened the door. Just as soon as I walked out

Sylvester jumped down on the floor and rushed over to me. We hissed a little at each other, and then did the usual smelling, and then just sat and stared.

Mrs. Cavanaugh said, "Now Sylvester, you mind your manners. You and Preacher Puss enjoy each other's company for a few minutes while Rosie and I chat, and then I'll have to grab Preacher Puss to take some measurements for her uniform." She then reached on the table beside her chair and picked up the bag of Whisker Lickin treats and after removing several she placed them on the floor. Sylvester and I rushed over immediately, we both could smell the treats as soon as they came out of the bag. We woofed them down quickly.....I think I got at least a couple more than Sylvester. After they were gone Sylvester swatted me with his paw, I guess because he thought I shouldn't have eaten so many. But I was polite and just sat and did not retaliate.

A few moments later Mrs. Cavanaugh said, "Okay Preacher Puss, time to get to work. If Rosie would place you on my dining room table I'll get the measurements I need in order to make you a real spiffy uniform."

Rosie carried me to the table and placed me there. Mrs. Cavanaugh had a sheet of paper and cloth measuring tape. As she took various measurements by wrapping the measuring tape around me she would then write them down on the paper. This went on for about ten minutes. In the meantime, I could just see in the living room and I noticed that Sylvester had jumped back up on the ledge close to the goldfish bowl and was intently watching Goldie as she swam circles.

Mrs. Cavanaugh said, "Okay Preacher Puss, I think I have what I need. You were a real good kitty. I might even find you some more Whisker Likins." Just as she said this I saw Sylvester leap to the table where the goldfish bowl was located. He immediately raised one paw and then raised his body up as he lowered the paw into the water trying to reach Goldie. The fish swam franticly to the bottom of the bowl. But then I saw the bowl start to tip over as Sylvester placed his weight on it. I knew that if the bowl was turned over the poor fish would die. I jumped as fast as I could, ran over to the goldfish bowl table, and then jumped up on it beside Sylvester. I placed my body against the bowl to keep it from turning over. Sylvester hissed loudly and then tried to swat me with his other front paw. When he did that, the paw that was in the bowl came out and he fell to the floor.

Rosie and Mrs. Cavanaugh had been watching. Mrs. Cavanaugh said, "Sylvester, you bad, bad cat.

I'm putting you outside. I told you to leave Goldie alone. No more cat treats for you." She rushed over and picked up Sylvester, carried him to the front door, and placed him outside.

Rosie said, "Mrs. Cavanaugh, I do believe I just saw Preacher Puss save the life of Goldie. If she hadn't jumped up there and pressed her body against the bowl it and Sylvester would both have fallen to the floor. And Goldie would likely have been a goner."

"You are absolutely correct, Rosie, that cat saved my Goldie!" exclaimed Mrs. Cavanaugh. She then pulled several more cat treats from the Whisker Lickin package and placed them on the floor beside me. I looked up at her with a thankful look, a big meow, and several appreciative tail swishes and then promptly woofed down all the cat treats.

"Well, all's well that ends well," Rosie said. "Do you think you have all the measurements you need for the uniform?"

Mrs. Cavanaugh replied, "Yes I think so, and the extra uniform you brought to me will certainly provide more material than I will need. I'll get started this afternoon. If everything goes well I should have it all ready by no later than this weekend. Do you think you might be able to bring Preacher Puss back over Sunday afternoon to try it on? If you could that would give us time to make any adjustments prior to the ceremony next Wednesday."

"That would work fine with me. I'll just take Preacher Puss home with me this weekend, and plan to bring her back here Sunday afternoon. Why don't we say 3 pm unless I hear from you otherwise?"

"Sounds perfect," replied Mrs. Cavanaugh. "And thanks again to Preacher Puss for saving my Goldie." She reached down and gave me several nice strokes. I like her a lot, but that Sylvester is not a good cat. I hope I don't even see him when I come back on Sunday.

CHAPTER 14
HARLAN, KENTUCKY

Friday morning

Bert, Kyle, and Fred were once again having coffee at Creech's Cafe. Bert said, "Okay Fred, everything is all set with the Slusher brothers to have our Preacher Puss deputizing ceremony at their farm next Wednesday at 2 pm. I talked with Gunsmoke and he said they would set up in the great room, and would have refreshments for everyone. He also said he'd try and round up as many of their cats as possible and have them there to play with Preacher Puss. Rosie will provide them with a list of all invited guests, and Charlie will use that list to admit people at the gate. So, I think everything is good from their end, now we need to contact the media that we wish to invite and to get the certificate printed up and framed. Rosie is having Mrs. Cavanaugh sew a deputy's uniform for Preacher Puss to wear. I don't know how that will go, but at least we can try. If she will wear it I'm sure the newspapers will get some real cute pictures for their articles. Here's the media list that I came up with....take a look and let me know if I've left anyone out."

Fred took the list from Bert:

Harlan Daily Enterprise
Knoxville News-Sentinel
Louisville Courier Journal
Lexington Herald-Leader
Lexington television station WKYT
Harlan radio station WHLN
Harlan radio station WFSR

After looking at the list Fred said, "I think you got 'em all. Likely not all of them will attend, but I'm sure enough will that we'll get real good coverage. I'll bet WKYT will send down Barbara Clark, since she's a Harlan native."

Bert replied, "Well, if you think that list is good, I'll pass it to Rosie to make the phone calls and prepare the list of names to submit to the Slusher brothers. Do you think you could take care of coming up with the framed document that we'll present?"

Fred said, "Not a problem at all. I'm pretty good with that kind of thing! I'll have the document read something like:

Because of her heroic acts in subduing criminals
The cat named Preacher Puss is hereby officially made
An honorary Harlan County, Kentucky deputy sheriff

And then it will be signed by you, as Harlan County Sheriff and by me, as Mayor of Harlan. How does that sound?"

Bert said, "Fred, you always did have a way with words! That would be perfect. Can you get it all printed up nicely, and then after we sign get it framed?"

"I'll have it all ready by no later than Monday. That be okay?"

"Absolutely," the sheriff replied.

Kyle then said, "Okay, now that we've disposed of the business at hand, how about sending us back to work with one of your latest stories, Fred?"

The mayor rubbed his chin, and after a few seconds of thought said, "I did hear a good one on the radio as I drove in to work this morning. They were talking about this fellow that went to see his doctor about his snoring problem. After examining the fellow, the doctor asked him if his snoring bothered his wife. He replied that it not only bothered his wife, but also the entire congregation!"

Bert and Kyle laughed loudly, and Kyle said, "I think that guy attends my church!"

•••

Bert handed Rosie the media list and said, "The mayor approved our inviting these. If you would be so kind as to do that and then prepare a list of everyone attending and pass it along to the Slusher brothers it would be a big help."

Rosie replied, "I'll get right on it. Shouldn't be a problem. In addition to the media names, I guess we only have the three of us, Mayor Knapp, and Preacher Puss?"

"Yeah, I believe that's it," Bert said. "Course there will be a bunch of folks from the Slusher farm there. I'm sure all seven of the Koreans will attend plus George and Ray. Charlie will have to stay on the gate. And then of course Gunsmoke and Booger will be there. So that would be a total of 11 from the farm, plus an unknown number of cats."

Kyle chuckled and said, "Yeah, lots and lots of cats!! Preacher Puss will be delighted."

I had been listening intently to all this, and it kept sounding better and better. I just can't wait for next Wednesday.

Just as Bert turned to start walking to his office the sheriff's department's entrance door opened and in walked Rosie's mom carrying her pet raccoon, Bandit.

Mom shouted to everyone, "Surprise, surprise!! Bandit and I decided to take a little outing for the weekend and we decided to come to Harlan!"

My eyes got big as saucers. I can't believe it. My buddy Bandit is here to visit with me! I jumped up from my usual prone position and announced my presence with a loud meow, and then jumped to the floor and over to Mom. She gently lowered Bandit and placed him beside me. We each raised a paw and touched them together, and then began to sniff each other thoroughly. Rosie came from behind her counter with Whisker Lickin treats in hand and placed several between us. We eagerly started to woof them down.

"Now isn't that just the sweetest sight you ever saw," Rosie said as she and her Mom hugged. "This is indeed a surprise. I didn't have any idea you were coming to Harlan, but I'm sure pleased you did."

Mom said, "Me and ole Bandit just got a little bored, and decided we wanted to get out for a day or two . . . and the drive to Harlan is only a little over two hours, and it was good trip. You think you can put us up for the weekend?"

"Of course," Rosie replied. "Your timing was perfect. Roy left this morning on a week-end fishing trip, so I've got the house all to myself. You and Bandit will be excellent company. I was already planning to take Preacher Puss home with me for the weekend. She has to return to see a seamstress on Sunday afternoon who's making her a cute little deputy sheriff's uniform to wear for a ceremony she'll be in next Wednesday. So she and Bandit will get to spend the weekend together. I'm sure they'll both enjoy that."

Bert and Kyle both looked down at me and Bandit and smiled. Bert said, "Well, I never thought I'd see the day that there was a coon in my office . . . but today's the day!" I swished my tail and meowed. Bandit just looked at Bert.

Mom said, "Well honey, if you'll give me the key to your house I think Bandit and I will go there and get a little rest. I'm not as young as I used to be, and I'm a tad tired from my trip. I'm sure Bandit will enjoy a nap as well, and then he'll be all ready to play with Preacher Puss when you two get home."

Bandit and I parted company with affectionate hisses as Mom took him and Rosie's house key and said, "We'll see you after work."

Mom then said to Bert and Kyle, "You boys keep the peace. It was good to see you." She then turned and walked out of the office.

Now I was not only looking forward greatly to my ceremony next Wednesday, but I can't wait to get to Rosie's house after work to visit with Bandit. What a lucky cat I am!

• • •

As Mom and Bandit left the Harlan County Court House Mom noticed two men sitting on the low court house wall talking. The two were Bennie Sekao and Ray Kidd.

Ray Kidd worked for the Slusher brothers. He, along with Charlie and George, had gone to high school with Gunsmoke and Booger. Years later, after the Slusher brothers became wealthy, they hired all three to work for them at their farm. Charlie and George were primarily responsible for working as guards at the farm's entrance gate. Charlie worked the first shift and George the second. Ray worked mostly running errands for the brothers. He did most of the grocery buying, bill paying, and any other chore requested by Gunsmoke or Booger.

After Ray graduated from high school he volunteered for the U.S. Army. Bennie Sekao also joined the army at the same time as Ray, although the two did not know each other. They first met when at boot camp, and then by chance both got assigned to duty at Fort Knox, Kentucky where they worked as tank mechanics. They became very close friends during their years in the service. After leaving the service each returned to Harlan County, but went their separate ways. Ray continued to work several different jobs in the Benham, Kentucky area before being recruited by the Slusher brothers, while Bennie fell victim to alcohol while working odd jobs in Harlan. The two now frequently ran into each other in Harlan, and when that happened they would sit for long periods of time reminiscing about their time in the army and talking about current events.

Today Bennie had been waiting for Ray. He knew that on Fridays Ray usually had errands to run in town and that he would likely park his car somewhere around the court house. And Bennie was right. As soon as Ray parked Bennie spotted him and shouted for him to come over and chat. Bennie knew this would be his best opportunity to find out a time when all the North Koreans at the farm would be there together.

After doing the chit-chat for about fifteen minutes Bennie said, "Ray, are all seven of those North Koreans still at the farm?"

"They sure are," replied Ray. "Why do you ask?"

"Just curious," Bennie said. "I just wondered if they would all elect to stick together and work for Gunsmoke and Booger or if they might want to move on."

Ray said, "They've all got it made at the farm. The brothers give them anything they want. They've got good shelter and food, and are paid good money. They work hard, and seem to really appreciate their situation. I really don't expect to see any of them ever leave."

"They participate in all the farm activities?" asked Bennie.

"Oh sure," replied Ray. "All seven are just like family to us. We see each other every day, and do all kinds of things together."

"So they've blended into life very nicely, I take it," Bennie said.

"Like I said, just like family," Ray replied.

Ray continued, "The big thing going on right now

is to get all set up for a ceremony that's scheduled for the farm next Wednesday at 2 pm. That cat in the sheriff's office is going to be made an honorary deputy. Can you believe that?"

Bennie perked up and said, "Really. Ole Preacher Puss is going to be made a deputy?"

"That's right," Ray said. "All kinds of media have been invited to cover it. It'll be all over the news. We're having the event in the great room of the farm house."

Bennie said, "You think those Koreans will be there too?"

Ray answered, "Funny you should ask, but certainly, I'm sure all of them will attend. They all love Preacher Puss, and wouldn't want to miss her big ceremony."

"I was just curious," Bennie said. "Personally, I'm not real fond of that cat. She has attacked me several times, and I've still got some scars to prove it!"

Ray laughed and said, "Yeah, I remember some of those incidents. I think they all involved you pulling guns out in the sheriff's office and she jumped you."

"That's not funny, Ray. That cat has claws you wouldn't believe. And she knows how to use 'em. I've come to finally learn that she just don't like guns," said Bennie.

"Well, Bennie, ole buddy, I guess I better take off and get my errands run. It's been great talking with you . . . as always," Ray said.

"Hey Ray, same here. You take care, and I'll see you around," Bennie said as Ray stood and walked away.

Bennie smiled and thought, *okay Mr. Lee. I'm already for my $800 tomorrow. I've got just the information you want.*

CHAPTER 15
HARLAN, KENTUCKY

Friday Afternoon

It had been a long afternoon for me. I was so excited that Mom had brought Bandit to Harlan, and I just couldn't wait to go to Rosie's house to play with him. I tried taking several naps to pass the time, but was just so excited I couldn't even sleep, and that's most unusual for me!

Sheriff Sterling walked from his office into the reception area and said, "Okay Rosie, looks like it's about time to call it a week. I know both you and Preacher Puss are anxious to get home to see your mother and that coon. Also, would you please do me a favor and take a few pictures of Preacher Puss in his uniform when you go to Mrs. Cavanaugh's on Sunday?"

If cats could blush I would. I'm already having second thoughts about the uniform. It's just embarrassing for a cat to wear such a thing! I know everyone's looking forward to seeing me in it, but I'm dreading it. I'll probably go along with it just to please everyone, but I'm sure not going to wear it other than to the Wednesday ceremony.

"Sure thing, Bert," Rosie replied. "I'll snap several pictures using my cell phone and send them to you. I'm sure they'll be priceless!"

Bert replied, "Great. I'll then be able to show them to Mayor Knapp and Kyle. I know they'll be anxious to see them as well. You and Preacher Puss have a great weekend."

Bert then walked toward the door and reached up and gave me several nice strokes on his way out. I meowed my approval loudly. I really like the sheriff.

"Okay Preacher Puss, it's time to get the show on the road," Rosie said as she came over and gathered me in her arms. "I think I've got everything all turned off for the weekend, and I did remember to get a couple bags of Whisker Lickins to take along for you and Bandit. So I guess we're good to go."

I heard those magic words, 'Whisker Lickins', and got even more excited. Not only was I going to be able to play with Bandit over the weekend, but we'd be given treats! Yep, I'm certainly ready to go!

The sheriff's office was on a very limited budget, mainly due to the decreasing population in Harlan

County. Many of its operations had been either eliminated or reduced. The office was only open Monday through Friday from 8 to 5. Several deputies remained on duty in their cruisers from 5 to 11 pm. From 11 pm to 8 am all calls going to the sheriff's office were redirected to the Kentucky State Police post 10 in Harlan.

With me in her arms, Rosie locked up the entrance door and headed for her car, looking forward to seeing her mom and Bandit.

•••

Mom greeted Rosie with a big hug when she walked in holding me. I immediately started squirming to get placed down so I could play with Bandit.

"Okay, okay," Rosie said as she placed me on the floor. "Go find your friend!"

I didn't have far to go. I saw Bandit in a corner of the living room staring at me with those big encircled eyes. I ran over and greeted him with an affectionate meow. He immediately stood and started sniffing me . . . we animals just love to do that.

Mom said, "Well ole Preacher Puss and Bandit seem very content now, so why don't we let them go outside to roam a little. I bet they both could use the exercise."

Rosie opened a package of Whisker Lickins, pulled several out in her hand, and walked over and placed them on the floor beside us. She said, "Here's a little treat for you two. After you've woofed them I'll let you out in the yard to play. It's completely fenced, so I know you'll be safe."

Rosie had her large back yard completed fenced with extra high wooden plank fencing so that she could allow Preacher Puss to play there without any fear of her getting out or of other cats or dogs getting in. Other than through the back door of her home, the only other entrance to the back yard was through a side gate which normally was closed and latched.

Although the neighborhood where Rosie lived was normally very quiet and peaceful, it did have one dog problem. About a quarter mile from Rosie's house was another that belonged to a man nicknamed Mean Jeb. He did not have a regular job, just did anything legal or illegal to pick up enough money to survive. He was constantly running into trouble with the law. In order to keep people from snooping around his home he had a vicious pit bull dog named Brutus. The dog had been trained by Mean Jeb to attack anyone or anything coming on his property. Brutus weighed about 75 pounds, barked almost constantly, and particularly loved to catch and kill squirrels or any other animal that invaded his territory. The big problem was that Brutus frequently escaped from Mean Jeb's home and terrorized neighbor's dogs and cats, and sometimes even the neighbors themselves. The police and animal control had been called many times, but Brutus was usually nowhere to be found by the time they arrived. He was a very mean dog, but also a smart one. He had been caught one time several months ago and spent a day at the dog pound until Mean Jeb came to his rescue. Today Brutus had again escaped.

Rosie and Mom walked from her living room through the hall to the back door which was off from the kitchen and dining room. Bandit and I trailed closely behind them. Rosie then opened the door and held it for us to go out. We gladly obliged. We bounded out into the spacious back yard and started checking everything out. It really felt good to be outdoors and able to exercise. We ran together, frequently stopping to smell anything of interest. Rosie had placed lots of cat toys around the back yard, and we both spent time playing with them.

The fun continued for about an hour. It stopped when Bandit and I heard a very loud and scary growl. We looked toward the gate and saw a sight that caused us both to freeze. There in the open gate stood the meanest looking dog I had ever seen. He was big. He was showing his very large teeth, and he was growling. Suddenly he began to run with amazing speed toward me and Bandit. Unfortunately for us, we were in a corner of the yard and it was pretty obvious to me that we couldn't outrun him. But that didn't matter anyway, because we were so scared we just watched him come pounding toward us. Bandit was on my left, and as the dog got closer it seemed to me he was going to first attack my friend. I just couldn't let that happen. I had to time it just right. My fur stood straight out, and I extended my claws. I remembered how in a previous encounter with a bear I was able to escape by digging my claws into his snout, so I thought I'd try that maneuver again. Just as the dog was almost to Bandit I jumped directly toward his nose with all four of my paws pointed toward his face. It was a good move. When my claws hit his nose and dug in the growling stopped and the howling started. The dog shook his head violently, trying to dislodge me. When he did it caused my claws to scrape across his nose and face, leaving deep cuts. Blood started spurting into his eyes, almost blinding him. I finally let go my grip and fell to the ground. The dog then turned and quickly ran back to the open gate and out.

I looked at Bandit. He was still shaking with fear.

Mom and Rosie had rushed out the back door when they heard the commotion. They had just started running toward us when they saw the dog go back through the open gate.

"Oh no," Rosie said. "Someone left that gate unlatched. It must have been the people who mow my grass. I told them to be sure the gate was latched, but I guess they failed to do it."

The two ladies bent over and picked us up. Rosie got me and Mom picked up Bandit. Rosie said, "You poor things, that old mean dog tried to fight you. From the looks of all the blood on his face I'd say my Preacher Puss got the best of him!"

I purred my approval. Bandit was still shaking visibly in Mom's arms. That dog really spooked him. Our weekend together was not off to a good start, but I knew it would get better.

Rosie walked over to the gate and locked the latch securely. She then placed me back down on the ground. Mom was still trying to comfort Bandit, and had him all cuddled up in her arms. His shaking had subsided, and she gently placed him down beside me. We sat together while the ladies returned into the house. I was glad they didn't see the dog come in and then my attacking him. It would likely have gotten them real upset. I was pleased things ended up as they did. The only damage was to the dog, and he deserved it!

CHAPTER 16
HARLAN COUNTY, KENTUCKY

Saturday morning

The three North Korean colonels were discussing their upcoming day's activities. They were seated in the living room of the Stepp farm house.

Colonel Lee said, "As far as I can determine everything has gone according to plan thus far. I think everything here is okay. I still am concerned about the Johnsons snooping around, but I really don't think they suspect anything....I believe they bought our story about evaluating the forests for timber rights, but we must continue to watch them carefully. I believe that Mr. Bennie Sekao will come up with a day and time for us when all the deserters will be at the Slusher brother's farm, and I'll learn that for sure at 4 pm today. And we've got the GPS coordinates for their home. In addition, the time we've spent for the last couple of days getting the chopper completely ready for the mission has gone well. So I do believe we're right on track."

"Are we still planning to do a dry run to the Slusher farm today?" asked Colonel Gim?

Colonel Lee replied, "Yes, I think we need that. I want to be absolutely sure that we know about how long it will take to get there, and that we can easily identify the farm house. We'll just follow our GPS coordinates, and it shouldn't be a problem. Yie will be flying with me as navigator, and Gim, you keep guard here and monitor our phone. If we encounter any problem we'll call. Is that agreeable?"

Colonels Yie and Gim nodded their heads in agreement.

•••

The Robinson helicopter lifted off. Colonel Lee, sitting in the left seat said to Colonel Yie through his microphone, "It's a beautiful day to fly. These Kentucky mountains are truly beautiful." He looked at the GPS instrument held in Colonel Yie's left hand and moved the cyclic to a course that would take them to the Slusher farm.

In only about 10 minutes the two saw a huge clearing ahead and a large home in its center. They were flying at an altitude of about 1000 feet and the GPS said they were only 3 miles from their target.

"I'll take it up to about 5000 feet to minimize the noise," Lee said. Yie gave a nod.

Colonel Lee then maneuvered the chopper directly over the Slusher farm house. As the two were looking down they noticed a person working in back of the home looking up toward them. Colonel Lee said, "Looks like we've been spotted. I'll get us out of here. We don't need the attention."

The Robinson helicopter's FAA identification tail numbers had been painted over so that the aircraft's origin could not be identified from them.

The helicopter quickly turned toward home and gained altitude and speed. They continued back to the Stepp farm without incident.

After landing Colonel Gim approached the other two North Koreans as they jumped down from the aircraft and said, "Did all go well?"

Yie replied, "It did. Only takes about 10 minutes to reach the target from here. We saw one person there that seemed to be watching us, but we're sure they couldn't ID us."

Lee added, "Yes, and so I think the next flight will be for real. All we need to know is a day and time that we can catch them all, and after my meeting this afternoon with Mr. Sekao I think we'll have that information."

"Howdy neighbors," the loud shout came from the tree line of the farm.

The three turned quickly toward the voice and saw the Johnson brothers walking toward them.

"We heard the racket that hell-e-copter was making and thought we'd just check and see if we could have our ride yet?" Billy Bob said as brother Bubba's head moved rapidly up and down with a big smile on his face.

Colonel Lee replied, "Good morning Johnsons. We're still on a tight schedule making our runs assessing the land for timber rights. It'll still be a little while before we can have the time to take you for your rides, but we will do it."

"Aw shucks," Bubba replied. "We been getting our hopes all up for it. It sure does look like fun!"

"Yes it will be," said Colonel Lee, "and we're looking forward to taking you up in it....we just need a little more time."

"Well, okay," Billy Bob replied. "We'll get back to our place....maw's got chores for us to do. You boys have a good day now, ya hear?"

"Yes, we hear," Colonel Lee replied as the Johnsons turned and started walking back to their home.

•••

Saturday afternoon

Colonel Lee found a parking spot very close to where he parked last Thursday when he came into town. Almost as soon as he got parked he saw Bennie on the court house lawn running toward his car. The colonel motioned for him to get in.

"Hey Mr. Lee," Bennie said as he entered the passenger seat. "I was watching for you."

Colonel Lee replied, "Yes, I see you were, Mr. Sekao, and I hope you have some good information for me."

"I sure do," Bennie replied. "I got a buddy named Ray that works at the Slusher farm. Ole Ray and me did a stint in the army together. He runs errands for the Slusher brothers, and I see him here in town frequently. I was watching for him yesterday, and sure enough, he came in to town and we got together. We did the chit chat for a while and then I got around to asking about the Koreans. Now if you've got my $800 I'll be happy to tell you what I found out."

Colonel Lee reached to the car's sun visor and retrieved the envelope. He passed it to Bennie and said, "I think you'll find eight one hundred dollar bills in there. Please tell me what you found out."

Bennie opened the envelope and counted the bills. He then said, "Right on the money. Okay, here's what I learned. There's a real strange cat that lives in the Harlan County Sheriff's office over there," he pointed across the street. "That ole cat, named Preacher Puss, is going to be made an honorary deputy sheriff at a ceremony to be conducted next Wednesday at 2 pm at the Slusher farm. They're going to invite a lot of media and present that cat with a certificate. All the Koreans will be there because they're real good friends with Preacher Puss, and Ray said they wouldn't miss it for the world."

Colonel Lee listened intently. He then nodded slowly and said, "I see. So you think that all seven of them will be present at this ceremony, and it will take place next Wednesday at 2 pm.....is that correct?"

"You got it," Bennie said. "Ray said it's a sure thing."

"Then you have indeed earned your money," the colonel said. "So that concludes our business. I thank you for your cooperation. Please do remember that all this is very confidential, and please don't discuss it with anyone."

"Mum's the word," Bennie said.

Colonel Lee then reached over and shook hands with Bennie and said, "It's been a pleasure Mr. Sekao."

Bennie said, "It has indeed Mr. Lee."

After Bennie had gotten out of the car Colonel Lee thought, *next Wednesday at 2 pm those seven deserters will get their reward.* He then drove off.

CHAPTER 17
HARLAN, KENTUCKY

Sunday Afternoon

Rosie and her mom had just arrived back home after going to church and then having lunch. Bandit and I had been allowed to play in the back yard. Rosie had double-checked the gate to make sure it was securely closed. We had really enjoyed being together again, and had spent the entire day yesterday playing both inside and outside the house. But I knew that the time was rapidly approaching when Mom and Bandit would have to go home, and that I would have to go with Rosie to Mrs. Cavanaugh's to try on my new uniform....and I really dreaded that!

Rosie opened the back door and walked into the yard. Bandit and I ran over to her, looked up, anticipating perhaps a few cat treats. Rosie did have several in her hand, and after placing them midway between Bandit and me she said, "Okay guys and gals, the time has come for us to leave. Mom and Bandit will drive separately and follow us to Mrs. Cavanaugh's home. Her house is on the way home for Mom and Bandit, so they'll stop there to see ole Preacher Puss in her new uniform. Mom said she wanted to take a picture of that."

I was already getting upset. I didn't even eat any of the cat treats, but Bandit didn't let them go to waste. This going to wear a uniform thing had completely taken my appetite. I just knew that both Bandit and that mean Sylvester would think I looked silly in it. Cats just don't wear clothes! But I guess I really don't have any choice . . . Rosie wants me to do it, so I guess I will. But I still won't like it.

Rosie and I pulled out first, and then Mom and Bandit followed in their car. It was about a 15 minute drive to Mrs. Cavanaugh's home.

• • •

Mrs. Cavanaugh and Sylvester were sitting in her living room awaiting Rosie and Preacher Puss. Mrs. Cavanaugh said to her cat, "Now Sylvester, I want you to be a real good kitty. You just play with Preacher Puss, and you two don't get into any meanness. And don't even think about getting anywhere near that fish bowl. Do you hear me?"

Sylvester continued to sit and swish his tail slowly back and forth.

Mrs. Cavanaugh looked out the window and saw two cars pull into her driveway. She got a puzzled look on her face and said, "Sylvester, there's another car out there behind Rosie. I wonder who it could be?"

She saw Rosie get out of her car carrying Preacher Puss, and then another lady got out of the other car also carrying something in her arms. The two started walking toward her house.

I looked at Bandit in Mom's arms. He looked scared. I'm sure he didn't know where he was going, or why. Rosie rang the door bell. Mrs. Cavanaugh opened it and said, "Welcome my friends. Do come in."

We entered and Rosie said, "Mrs. Cavanaugh, I would like you to meet my mother and her friend, Bandit."

Mrs. Cavanaugh patted Mom on the shoulder, looked at Bandit and said, "Now how sweet is that? Please do come on in and have a seat."

With that Rosie placed me on the floor, and Mom started to unwrap the blanket from around Bandit.

As soon as my paws hit the floor I started looking for Sylvester. I knew there would be trouble. I spotted him sitting on the floor under the front window. He was watching intently . . . I'm sure very curious about the creature Mom had in her arms.

Mom finished unwrapping Bandit and then placed him on the floor not far from me. I saw Sylvester's eyes get really big and his fur start to stick straight out. I knew exactly what he was thinking.....*I cannot believe there's a coon in my house!* He then lowered his head and started running as fast as he could directly toward Bandit. Rosie saw him first and shouted, "Sylvester's going to attack Bandit." She pointed toward the charging cat.

Mrs. Cavanaugh was on the other side of the room and couldn't get to her cat in time to stop him. She shouted, "Stop Sylvester! You stop immediately."

It was up to me. I was the only one who could stop Sylvester before he collided with Bandit. And if that happened, I knew my friend would be severely harmed. I had to time it just right. I got all set to pounce, and just as Sylvester flew toward Bandit I jumped immediately between them. Sylvester wasn't expecting it, and his head hit the middle of my body before he could get his paws up to break the impact. I felt a pain in my side as his head dug into my tummy. His scream was muffled by all my fur in his face, but the impact caused me to scream as well. I felt like I had been hit by a freight train.

Bandit ran to Mom and she scooped him up off the floor. Mrs. Cavanaugh finally got to Sylvester, grabbed him up, and said, "You mean, mean old cat. I'm putting you outside and I may never let you in again. You just cannot be good." She walked with him to the door, opened it, placed him outside, and said, "I'm really sorry for Sylvester's behavior. I just don't know what got into him."

Rosie reached down and picked me up. She petted me and said, "That's okay Mrs. Cavanaugh. I'm sure the sight of a raccoon in your house was just more than Sylvester could take. We should have warned you ahead of time. I think Preacher Puss will be fine. She just had the wind knocked out of her."

I purred my agreement, and swished my tail. I was already feeling better knowing that Sylvester wouldn't be around to see me in my uniform. Bandit would still see me, but maybe he would understand.

Bandit and I both got placed again on the floor.

Mrs. Cavanaugh brought refreshments for the ladies, and they did the chit-chat for several minutes.

Rosie and Mom took turns telling Mrs. Cavanaugh the story of how Bandit and I became friends. Finally Mrs. Cavanaugh said to Rosie, "Well, that's some story. You really should call the *Enterprise* and get a reporter to write a feature article about the two friends."

"Not a bad idea . . . I'll think about that. Now, is her uniform ready?" replied Rosie.

Mrs. Cavanaugh said, "It sure is. I was real pleased with it. I just hope it fits her well. I'll go get it."

Mrs. Cavanaugh walked into her sewing room, retrieved the uniform, brought it back into the living room and said, "Okay, Deputy Preacher Puss. Get up here on the dining room table and let's get this uniform on you."

I wasn't going to volunteer to jump up on the table, so Rosie grabbed me and placed me there. She said, "Now Preacher Puss, I want you to be good. Mrs. Cavanaugh has worked hard to make this nice uniform for you, so please let us try it on you."

Rosie is so good to me. I just couldn't object.

It took several minutes for them to get my legs in all the right holes and to get my head through the right place. There were buttons then on the front that had to be secured. Mrs. Cavanaugh had also incorporated a cap that was attached to the top-front of the uniform and flipped over my head. It had holes in it to let my ears stick out, and had a badge on the cap's front. After lots of tugging and adjusting, it was finally pronounced to be on. The three ladies then all stood back and looked at me.

"Just you look at that sweet thing," Mom said. "Let me grab my cell phone to take a picture. I never in my entire life saw anything like that!"

Now I know cats can't blush, but that's the way I was feeling. Then I looked down and saw Bandit looking at me with those big encircled eyes of his. I just knew he had to be laughing at me.

Mrs. Cavanaugh said, "If I do say so myself, I think it's a perfect fit. And a mighty fine looking deputy sheriff she is."

Rosie giggled and said, "Mrs. Cavanaugh, you've really outdone yourself. I think you've created the perfect feline deputy sheriff uniform."

I happened then to look toward the living room. And there in the window sat Sylvester looking in. He was sitting on the outside ledge under the window, and he looked for all the world like he had a big smirk on his face. I just know he thought I looked silly. I was embarrassed.

Rosie got her cell phone and joined Mom and Mrs.

Cavanaugh in taking pictures of me. They must have taken at least a dozen each. I was ready to get out of this uniform!

"Okay, Preacher Puss," Rosie said. "You've been a real good kitty. We'll get your uniform off and then you and Bandit will get some Whisker Lickins for being so good."

I think the part about getting out of the uniform sounded even better than going to get cat treats. But both were certainly welcome.

After Bandit and I woofed our cat treats Rosie paid Mrs. Cavanaugh for making my uniform and then we all said our good-byes. As we left the house I tried to stick my tongue out at Sylvester, but I'm not sure he saw me. At least that was over, and I only have to wear the uniform one more time . . . next Wednesday.

CHAPTER 18
HARLAN, KENTUCKY

Monday Morning

Bennie Sekao had a terrible headache. He was sitting on the Harlan County Court House wall. He didn't really remember for sure, but thought he had a little too much to drink and passed out here sometime yesterday. After he had received his final $800 payment on Saturday from Mr. Lee he headed straight to the local bootlegger and purchased a good supply of booze. From that time until now his memory was very fuzzy. He was staring directly into the morning sun, and that certainly didn't help his headache.

He continued to sit and think about his encounter with Mr. Lee. Something just didn't seem right about it. First of all, the guy clearly was Asian. Secondly, he paid me a lot of money and wanted me to keep quiet about it. And lastly, it sure seemed strange that he kept saying he had to know when all the North Koreans would be together at the Slusher Farm. And Bennie clearly remembered that attempts had been made previously on those North Koreans' lives. What if he had provided information to a killer who wanted to kill not only the Koreans but also maybe the Slusher Brothers and their employees, including his good friend Ray. Bennie shook his head....trying to shake away the cobwebs. He knew he had promised Mr. Lee that he would not tell anyone about their deal, but if something bad happened as a result of the information he gave Mr. Lee he'd never be able to forgive himself. He might be a drunk, but he knew he couldn't betray his friends. He knew what he had to do. He stood up, staggered a bit, and then started walking toward the sheriff's office.

•••

I was really enjoying my mid morning nap. I had finally recovered from the experience at Mrs. Cavanaugh's yesterday afternoon, and was snoozing on my shelf when I heard the door open and someone walked in. I opened one eye to see who it might be.

Rosie said, "Well, well, if it isn't ole Bennie Sekao. What brings you to the sheriff's office this morning Bennie?"

Then I recognized him! I knew this guy. He had been in here several times, and usually had some kind of gun, and I had attacked him each time. I'm sure he remembered me.

Bennie said, "Hi Rosie. I need to see the sheriff. I think I have some information that he needs to know."

"Okay, Bennie," Rosie replied. "Please just have a seat and I'll check to see if Bert can see you."

"Thanks Rosie," Bennie said.

Thank goodness he doesn't seem to have a gun this morning. I guess I won't have to attack him. I slowly closed my open eye and went back to dreaming. Seeing Bennie reminded me of my encounter with him at a meeting a couple of years ago in the City Hall. Someone had paid Bennie to disrupt the meeting by 'mooning' everyone. His appearance caused quite a commotion, and was reported in the *Enterprise* by a reporter that was present. I remember the article well:

> At exactly 10 am I was watching the beautiful cat that Deputy Cain had by her side. The cat sat very alert to all that was going on. Suddenly ole Bennie, the town drunk, appeared at the top of the stairs. Bennie walked into the back of the meeting room, turned around, dropped his pants

and underwear, and then bent over to 'moon' everyone. He appeared to then take a deep breath and was getting ready to yell something when the cat noticed his testicles swinging like a pendulum. The cat's eyes got real large and she pointed her head right at the testicles. I saw her claws come out, and then she lunged and made a hard swipe at them that struck home. The next sound was Bennie's ear piercing scream as he leaped forward to escape the cat. In doing so he lost his balance and went head over heels down the stairs. There was then another scream as his head bounced off one of the stairs. The EMTs hauled him off to the hospital with a fractured skull.

I had to chuckle. That was really funny, although I'm sure ole Bennie didn't think so. I believe he was in the hospital several days recovering from my attack. I again opened one eye to check on him. I guess he had heard me purring because he was looking straight at me with a real mean look on his face.

"I see you still got that damn cat," Bennie said to Rosie as she reentered the front office after conferring with the sheriff.

"She's still here on duty," Rosie replied. "And

she's going to be honored this Wednesday with a big ceremony at the Slusher Farm where she'll be made an official honorary deputy sheriff. I had Mrs. Cavanaugh make her a uniform to wear for it. The media will be there and take pictures . . . she'll look so cute."

Bennie said, "Yeah, I was talking with Ray Kidd a few days ago and he told me about it."

"Bert said for you to come on back....he'll be happy to talk with you," Rosie said.

"Thanks," Bennie replied as he stood and started walking toward the sheriff's office.

"Welcome Bennie," Bert said as he stood and the two shook hands. "Please have a seat and tell me what I can do for you."

Bennie sat and said, "Well Bert, my conscious been bothering me. As you know, I tip the bottle more than I should, but I do care about my town and my friends. And something happened last Saturday that just doesn't smell right to me, and I thought the best thing to do would be to come and tell you about it. It might be nothing, but it might not be. I figured if I told you then you could figure it out."

"Sounds serious, Bennie," the sheriff replied. "Please do tell me."

Bennie then told Bert about Mr. Lee's approaching him to get information about when all of the North Koreans at the Slusher farm would be together.

"You say this Mr. Lee was Asian?" Bert said.

"Looked that way to me," replied Bennie. "As a matter of fact, he looked almost exactly like the Koreans at Gunsmoke and Booger's farm. Yeah, I'm sure he was Asian."

"That is interesting . . . and troubling," Bert said. "I know you are aware that in the past attempts have been made to kill the North Koreans. And because of that, the FBI told me to keep close tabs on them and to report any suspicious activity. And this does sound suspicious."

Bennie said, "Oh boy, I hope I'm not in trouble with the FBI."

"No, no," the sheriff said, "not at all. As a matter of fact, if it does turn out to be something they might even have a reward for you."

"That's a relief and makes me feel much better," Bennie replied.

"Do you know where this Mr. Lee is staying or anything else about him?" Bert asked.

"No, nothing at all, except he drives a brown Chevrolet...maybe a couple of years old," said Bennie, and then added, "Oh, and he also said that I was recommended by Trigger Green."

Bert then wrote down a detailed description of Mr. Lee as given him by Bennie and said, "Bennie, I truly appreciate your telling me this. You certainly did the right thing. Your conscious should now be clear. But I would really appreciate it if you would keep an eye out for Mr. Lee, and if you see him let me know asap.... would you do that?"

"You bet, Bert," Bennie replied. "If I see him I'll run and tell you."

Bert stood and shook hands again with Bennie as he turned and left the office.

"Good to see you Bennie," Rosie said as he walked toward the door.

Bennie replied, "Thanks Rosie. Good to see you, but not that Preacher Puss there." He pointed at me.

Cats don't growl, but I did hiss a little at him. He hurried out the door.

•••

An hour later

Bert sat with Fred in Creech Cafe. Fred proudly displayed the certificate to be presented to Preacher Puss on Wednesday. He said, "Got it all ready, Bert. It just needs your signature...as you can see, I've already signed it."

Bert said, "It's a beauty, Fred." He pulled out a pen and signed the certificate. "I sure appreciate your putting it together. And I bet the certificate will go in that frame you have there."

Fred replied, "You got it." He slipped the certificate in the frame, and then held it out for them both to see.

"I know old Preacher Puss can't read, but I'm sure she'll be real proud of this," Bert said.

"Glad to do it. That cat has brought a lot of attention to Harlan, and everything has been very positive. She's a very good citizen, and she deserves the recognition," replied Fred.

The sheriff said, "Okay, we got that all ready, and I know Rosie has contacted the media, and they all said they planned to attend the ceremony. So it should get a lot of press. Now that we've got that all settled, I wanted to tell you about a visit I had just this morning from our friend Bennie Sekao."

Bert then filled in Fred about Bennie's story.

"So have you contacted the FBI about it?" asked Fred.

"Yeah, just got off the phone with them a few minutes ago. They seemed glad to get the information, and said they would increase their security around the Slusher farm....especially on Wednesday. Also, they said they wanted to meet with everyone at the farm tomorrow morning to see if they could uncover any other suspicious activity. And they requested that I be at that meeting as well. I'll keep you posted," Bert said.

"I sure hope it turns out to be nothing," replied the mayor. "That has potential for some bad publicity as well as possible harm. We don't need either. So, what are you going to do now?"

"As I told you, Bennie said that the mysterious Mr. Lee told him he was sent by Trigger Green. So I'm leaving here headed for Maggard's Grocery to have a talk with Trigger to see if he might have anything on Mr. Lee that he'd share with me." Bert said. "But before I go, I just know you might have a good story that will send me on my way with a smile!"

Fred thought a moment, and said, "Well, I did hear one on the radio this morning. Two police officers responding to a domestic disturbance with shots fired arrived on the scene. After discovering the wife had shot her husband for walking across her freshly mopped floor, they call their sergeant, and the conversation went something like this:

Policeman: Hello Sarge.

Sergeant: Yes?

Policeman: It looks like we have a homicide here.

Sergeant: What happened?

Policeman: A woman has shot her husband for stepping on the floor she had just mopped.

Sergeant: Have you placed her under arrest?

Policeman: No sir. The floor is still wet!

Bert got a huge smile. He stood, shook hands with Fred, and said, "Just what I needed Fred. Thanks. I'll be off to see Trigger Green. You be sure to bring that framed certificate to the ceremony on Wednesday."

"Will do," Fred replied. "Give ole Trigger my regards."

•••

Fatso looked up when the doorbell jingled. He said, "Hey Bert, good to see Harlan County's finest. You doing okay?"

Bert walked over to the counter beside Fatso, shook hands, and said, "Doing well, Fatso, but I need to chat with Trigger. I hope I caught him."

"You did indeed," replied Fatso. "But before I unlock the door, you gotta tell me what is brown, has four legs, and a trunk?"

Bert thought a moment and said, "Haven't heard that one before. Got me."

Fatso replied, "A mouse coming back from vacation!"

"Of course," the sheriff replied with a chuckle, "I should have known."

Fatso then pressed the button under the counter to unlock the door to Trigger Green's office in the back of the grocery. Bert turned and started walking toward it.

Responding to the knock on his door, Trigger Green jumped up from his desk and shouted, "Come on in."

The two greeted each other and then took seats.

Trigger said, "Bert, I always welcome your visits. But I'll guess you're not here on a social call."

Bert replied, "You are perceptive, Trigger. I know you realize that I greatly value you as a friend and as a citizen of Harlan County. Obviously I don't agree with most of the kinds of things you're into, but I respect you and feel that you always put the welfare of people first."

"That's pretty good pussyfooting Bert," replied Trigger. "Tell me what you think I can do for you."

"I had a visit earlier today from Bennie Sekao. He told me a story about how he had been employed by a Mr. Lee to snoop on the activity at the Slusher farm and to find out when all of the North Koreans there would be together during daylight hours. This Mr. Lee told Bennie that you had recommended him for the job. After hearing the story, it certainly sounded very suspicious. I've contacted the FBI and they're on it. But I thought you might be able to help me. Could you tell me anything additional about this Mr. Lee?"

Trigger thought for a moment and said, "Bert, I gotta be careful. I think you can appreciate that. But the information you just told me about what Mr. Lee wanted from Bennie is concerning to me. I had no idea what his business was, he just explained he needed a contact in Harlan. He said the contact needed to be generally aware of what was going on in the county, not particularly bright, and would work for money and keep his mouth shut. I immediately thought of Bennie, and recommended him. I guess I was wrong about his keeping his mouth shut."

The sheriff smiled and said, "Bennie just told me his conscious was bothering him. He said he didn't want to see anyone get hurt."

"Bennie does have a good heart," Trigger said. "I can understand that."

After thinking a bit longer Trigger continued, "There is one additional thing I will share with you, confidentially of course. Mr. Lee also asked for directions to the Slusher farm. He said he had a confidential matter he needed to discuss with them, and said he would deliver a note to Charlie at the gate. I didn't see anything wrong with that, so Fatso gave him the directions. That's everything I can recall about our meeting. I do hope you'll not have to tell anyone where you got this information."

"No problem, Trigger. I'll keep a lid on it, and I certainly appreciate your help," Bert replied.

After exchanging a few more pleasantries, Bert left Trigger's office and was walking back through the grocery store as Fatso shouted to him, "Hey Bert, you know what the elephant said to the naked man?"

Bert kept walking.

Fatso shouted, "The elephant said to the naked man: I just don't see how you can breathe through that little thing!"

Bert started laughing so hard he almost stumbled as he left the store.

CHAPTER 19
HARLAN COUNTY, KENTUCKY

Tuesday Morning

"Hey Charlie, how you doing?" Bert asked after coming to a stop at the Slusher Brothers' farm gate.

"Morning sheriff," Charlie replied through the open window in his guard house. "You go right on in. Special agents Clair Eaton and Rose McKay arrived just a few minutes ago. They should already be in the house."

Bert said, "Thanks Charlie. See you later."

Charlie said, "You will, in just a few minutes. Those FBI agents wanted all Slusher personnel present for their meeting, so Gunsmoke called me and said to leave my post and come to the house at 9:30. I'll see you then."

Bert looked at his watch. It was 9:10. He closed his window and drove on toward the farm house.

• • •

Everyone from the Slusher farm was gathered in the house's great room. All seven of the North Koreans, Charlie, George, Ray, Gunsmoke, and Booger, along with Sheriff Sterling and FBI Special Agents Clair Eaton and Rose McKay were all assembled, sitting around the room in very comfortable chairs and sofas. Most of the Koreans had cats in their laps, which they constantly stroked. After about ten minutes of small talk Bert stood, walked to the center of the room, and said

"I think we have everyone present, and I want to thank you for your cooperation. I think each of you already have met Agents Eaton and McKay, so introductions are not necessary. We'll make this meeting as short as possible so you can get back to your activities."

Bert then described his meeting with Bennie, and disclosed the fact that he knew from a reliable source that Mr. Lee had asked directions to the Slusher farm. He then asked if Agent Eaton would take it from there.

Clair Eaton stood and thanked the sheriff and everyone else for their cooperation, and then said, "As you all are well aware, North Korea's Supreme Leader Kim Jong-un has previously directed several attacks on you North Koreans in an effort to get revenge for your defecting. Thankfully, all those efforts were unsuccessful. The sudden appearance of Mr. Lee, who has been described as looking very much like a North Korean, and his inquiry about when he could be sure all seven of you Koreans would be here together, and then asking for directions on how to get here.....all this seems very suspicious. Unfortunately, we only know that Mr. Lee drives a brown Chevy....maybe two or three years old, and we do have a description of him."

At this point Agent Eaton passed out sheets to everyone that contained Mr. Lee's description.

She then continued, "The purpose of this meeting is to let everyone know about this person and his activity, and to ask if any of you have noticed anyone or anything out of the ordinary recently that could possibly be related."

Charlie held up his hand.

Agent Eaton said, "Yes Charlie, speak."

Charlie said, "Well, I don't know for sure, but I'm pretty sure it was last Thursday a car pulled up to the gate, and I do think it was a brown Chevy, and when I asked the driver his business he said he was a lost tourist looking for a place to take pictures of the mountains. The driver fits the description of Mr. Lee. When I told him this was private property and he would have to look elsewhere he simply smiled and thanked me and left."

Agent Eaton said, "Very interesting. Would your security camera have any pictures that might be useful? Maybe a license tag number, or picture of the driver?"

Charlie said, "Possibly. I'll check."

"Please do," said Agent Eaton. "Anyone else think of anything?"

Bin Yo-han then raised his hand.

"Yes Bin," Agent Eaton said.

Bin replied, "A few days ago I was working in the back yard and I noticed a helicopter flying directly above our house. It was a rather strange looking helicopter. Very small. It left quickly after I noticed it. The only other thing I remember about it was that I could see no identification markings on it."

Agent Eaton said, "Most interesting. Has anyone else noticed any helicopters lately?

All nodded negatively.

"Does anyone have anything else to report?" she asked.

Again, all nodded negatively.

Agent McKay then raised her hand.

"Yes, Rose." Agent Eaton said.

Rose McKay replied, "I would suggest that we might wish to immediately put out an all-points bulletin to both the police community and the media asking that anyone noticing a person of Mr. Lee's description driving a brown Chevrolet, or anyone noticing any unusual helicopter activity in Harlan County, to contact Sheriff Sterling immediately."

Agent Eaton said, "Great idea, Rose. Would you please take the responsibility to put that bulletin together and get it out immediately. It would be great to have it on the noon television and radio news programs."

"Will do," replied Agent McKay.

Clair Eaton then said, "If no one has anything else we'll conclude our meeting. Again, I thank each of you for your cooperation."

As the FBI agents and Sheriff Sterling were walking to their cars Agent Eaton said, "That was a great meeting. We got two very good pieces of information. The helicopter thing scares me a little. I'm going to ask for an immediate surveillance plane to fly over the county looking on the ground and in the air for helicopters matching the description given by Bin. Also, I'm going to bring in one of our guys tomorrow with a drone. I'll ask him to put it up at about 1,000 feet and constantly scan the area with a video camera. He'll monitor what the camera sees from his station on the ground. If he spots a helicopter or any other suspicious activity he'll call me immediately."

"Sounds good," Bert replied. "Thanks for helping us on this. I sure hope tomorrow will go smoothly."

The two agents nodded in agreement.

• • •

30 minutes later

Bert had just gotten back to his office when his cell phone rang, "Sheriff Sterling here."

"Hi Sheriff, this is Agent Eaton. I just had a phone call from Charlie, and he said he reviewed the security tape carefully and could not give us any new information. He said the guy backed up a good ways from the gate before turning around, and then there was a piece of cardboard covering his license plate. Charlie said he didn't notice it at the time, but that it was clearly visible on the tape. So that was our man, but we have nothing new. I just sent a bulletin to all the police units and to the media, so they should be getting that word out. We'll keep our fingers crossed that someone sees something."

Bert replied, "Thanks Clair, I appreciate your letting me know. I'll see you tomorrow afternoon.

•••

Noon

The three North Korean colonels were having their lunch in the kitchen of the Stepp farm house. A radio sitting on the refrigerator was turned on and tuned to Harlan radio station WHLN.

Colonel Lee said, "I sure will be glad when this things over. I'm beginning to get the feeling that the authorities may suspect something. Certainly we've been very careful, but I just have a feeling that the drunk who provided me the information on the defectors may not have kept his mouth shut. It's just a feeling. Otherwise, I do think everything is all set for tomorrow. Yie and I will leave on our mission at exactly 2 pm. Since it only takes a few minutes to reach the target everyone should be assembled by then for their ceremony in the farm house. Gim will monitor our radio for any unexpected activity."

Colonel Yie held up a finger to his mouth, indicating silence. They heard the announcer on the radio say:

Our station has just received a bulletin from the Federal Bureau of Investigation. It asks that all Harlan County citizens be on the alert for a brown Chevy sedan. The car is a couple of years old and is driven by an Asian. Also, the FBI asks that any helicopter activity in the county be reported to them immediately. The reason for these requests is not stated. Anyone spotting the car or helicopters should call WHLN immediately and we will notify the FBI.

Colonel Lee jumped up from his chair and said, "Let's get the helicopter back in the barn. They likely will have aircraft out trying to spot us."

The three ran outside. Gim started the forklift, picked up the pallet from the bed of the semi truck, took it outside and placed it in position for the helicopter. Lee jumped in the Robinson R22, quickly started it up, lifted off and moved in position over the pallet, and sat it down. Gim then moved the pallet and helicopter back into the semi in the barn.

After closing the barn doors the three started walking back to the house. Colonel Lee said, "I just hope they haven't previously spotted it. If not, we should be safe until tomorrow. We'll plan to move the aircraft back out just moments before we launch."

• • •

The Johnsons were also having their lunch. They sat huddled around their kitchen table, and they too were listening to the radio while eating. When they heard the announcement they each stopped eating and looked at each other. Maw said, "Boys, you just heared what was said. The FBI's lookin for a hell-e-copter and a brown Chevy. Them hell-e-copters is scarce as hen's teeth around these parts. And we knows where one is. And you boys said them Chi-nee-men drives a brown Chevy too."

"What should we do, Maw," Billy Bob asked.

Maw thought a moment, and said, "Well, we gotta do our duty. If the FBI wants us to report it....then seems that's what we should do."

Bubba replied, "Yeah, Maw, I agree. But we don't want to get them Chi-nee-men in trouble. They told us they was just flying that thing around looking for good timber. If we goes and tells the FBI and they cause trouble for the Chi-nee-men they likely would think ill of us. They is our neighbors. Maybe we should investigate a little first . . . and try and see if they are who they say they are."

Maw thought and said, "Bubba, you got a brain in that there head of yours. I think you're right. Why don't you boys mosey over to the Stepp farm and do a little snooping. I won't call WHLN until I hears back from youins."

"Okay Maw," replied Billy Bob. "But we gonna finish lunch first. Me and Bubba will check out them Chi-nee-men first thing after lunch. I shore hope they be okay. Otherwise, we won't be able to get our hell-e-copter rides."

• • •

2 pm

Sheriff Sterling, Kyle, and Fred were enjoying their afternoon coffee at Creech Cafe. Fred asked, "Have you boys heard anything as a result of the media announcements that were aired at noon?"

Kyle replied with a chuckle, "We got one phone call. The FBI called us and said someone called WHLN to report a brown Chevy driven by a foreigner. They got his license plate number. We checked it and found it belonged to the owner of the Mexican restaurant!"

Fred laughed and said, "Well, I guess that didn't help any."

Bert said, "No, it sure didn't. And I really don't expect to get any help from the announcements. Whoever this Lee fellow is, he's not stupid. I'm sure he's covered his tracks. So it leaves me very worried about tomorrow. I'm certainly glad the FBI is working with us on this, but we can only do so much."

Fred answered, "Bert, you've done everything you can do. I think things will go well at the ceremony tomorrow."

Kyle said, "I know what would really help us right now, Fred. Why don't you cheer us up with one of your stories."

Fred thought for a moment and said, "I did read an interesting article in the *Enterprise* this morning. You guys know all this stuff on the news about the Russians these days. The article was about a race that was recently held in Russia. Originally it was supposed to have about a dozen men running in it, but at race time only two showed up. One was Russian, one was American. They ran the race and the American won. The next day the Russian newspapers reported the results. They said, *In the big race yesterday the Russian finished second and the American was next to last!"*

Bert and Kyle laughed, and Bert said, "I guess that's what you call Fake News!"

• • •

Bubba and Billy Bob had walked to the Stepp farm. They had arrived at the tree line that surrounded the farm house and barn. They had taken a seat on a rock, and were still hidden from view by the trees and bushes. They sat and watched the house and barn, and saw nothing. Bubba said, "Billy Bob, you notice anything different?"

"No, can't say that I do," replied Billy Bob.

Bubba said, "You better get your eyes checked. Where's that hell-e-copter?"

"You right, brother, it's missing. And we ain't heard no noise from it, so it likely ain't up in the air," Billy Bob replied.

"You reckon them Chi-nee-men done left?" asked Bubba.

"Don't rightly know," said Billy Bob. "Sure ain't seen hide nor hair of em. I think everything's too quiet."

Bubba spoke, "Well, Maw told us to snoop. So snoop's what we should do."

Billy Bob replied, "We is snooping. What you got in mind?"

"Well, maybe we should first walk down the driveway to where they been parking their car. See if it's there," said Bubba.

"Okay," replied Billy Bob. The two brothers then walked through the trees to where the driveway intersected them and then proceeded to walk down the driveway toward the road. At the end of the driveway the brown Chevy was parked, blocking anyone from entering.

"Well, it's still here," Bubba said.

"Yeah," his brother replied. "I got me a pencil and piece of paper here. I'm gonna write down their license plate number. Maw can report it if we tell her to."

"Good thinking," Bubba said. The two then started walking back up the driveway toward the farm house. Bubba continued, "Billy Bob, there's just one place that hell-e-copter could be."

Bubba said, "You right brother. If they ain't flying it then it's got to be in the barn."

Billy Bob said, "So I guess we snoop next in the barn?"

"Sounds bout right to me," replied Bubba.

After the brothers came to the part of the driveway that could be seen from the farm house they retreated into the woods and continued in them until they reached a point where the barn stood between them and the farm house.

Bubba said, "Okay Billy Bob, I think now we can walk from here to the barn without any of them Chi-nee-men seeing us from the house." The two started walking toward the barn.

Billy Bob opened the man-door at the back of the barn and the two walked inside.

They saw the truck parked facing them, and walked around it to the front of the barn. They then looked back into the open rear doors of the semi. "Well, I guess that answers the question," Bubba said as the two looked at the helicopter parked in the semi on top of the pallet.

"Shore does," Billy Bob replied. "I ain't no detective, but it shore does look like them Chi-nee-men might be who the FBI's looking for."

"I think we done snooping," said Bubba. "Let's head home and tell Maw what we found."

"You're going nowhere," a voice said from behind them.

The brothers turned around quickly, and to their surprise saw all three North Koreans pointing guns at them.

"Does this mean we don't get to go for our ride in your hell-e-copter?" asked Bubba.

Colonel Lee smiled and said, "That is correct. Now please turn back around and put your hands behind your backs."

Yie and Gim then each tied ropes around the brothers' wrists.

Colonel Lee said, "Okay, lets walk to the house."

The five men walked to the house. Once inside the Koreans took the brothers to a bedroom and made them sit on the floor beside the bed. They then wrapped ropes around each brother's waist and then around a bed post such that each was tied with their backs to the bed, one on each side.

"We won't put gags on your mouths unless we hear you talking. Please remain quiet. Screaming won't help . . . there's no one but us to hear." Colonel Lee said.

Billy Bob replied, "We'll be quiet. We shore had you guys figured all wrong."

"You just keep quiet, and after we've left tomorrow someone will find you and you will be okay," said Colonel Lee.

The three Koreans walked out of the bedroom and closed the door. They then walked back into their living room and took a seat.

Colonel Yie said, "Lee, it was real lucky you happened to spot those two as they came up the driveway headed into the trees. Otherwise, they might have damaged the chopper and the mission could have ended."

"Very lucky," Colonel Lee replied. "I just happened to look out the window and saw them. Maybe that's a sign lady luck will be with us."

"Hopefully, but what about their mother? She certainly will miss them and be concerned. She could well contact the police," said Colonel Gim.

"I think that's just a chance we have to take," said Colonel Lee. "If she hasn't already contacted them perhaps she will wait until they return. If our luck runs good she won't figure out that something's wrong until tomorrow afternoon, and our mission will have been completed. I think we should not try going to their house and capturing her . . . these mountain people have lots of guns and know how to use them. If she saw us approaching her home she likely would start shooting at us. I don't think we would want that."

The other two Koreans nodded in agreement.

Colonel Lee continued, "Let's just keep our weapons at the ready and watch for anything. Hopefully we'll be able to just sit tight until 2 pm tomorrow. We'll then carry out our mission and head back home."

•••

9 pm

Maw Johnson had just finished washing the dishes after she had supper. She thought to herself, *Those boys are certainly running late. True, I didn't tell them how long to snoop, but I figured they'd get hungry and be back here for supper. I could call the police and report what we know, but I'd sure rather have the information the boys get from their snooping before I call. I guess I'll just wait till tomorrow....it's too late now for anything to be done today anyway. If the boys don't show up by noon tomorrow I'll call and report them missing and pass along the information we know about the hell-e-copter and the brown Chevy.*

CHAPTER 20
HARLAN COUNTY, KENTUCKY

Wednesday morning

Sheriff Sterling was very concerned that no additional information had been uncovered as a result of the FBI's media releases yesterday. He knew that Mr. Lee was out there somewhere, and he strongly suspected he had something planned for today's ceremony at the Slusher farm. He thought he'd drive out this morning to talk again with Trigger Green to see if he might think of something else that would help.

"Good Morning Fatso," Bert said has he walked in the door at Maggard's Grocery.

"Hey Sheriff," Fatso replied. "Little early for you to be out isn't it?"

"Early bird gets the worm, so they say," the sheriff replied.

"I bet it's Trigger you want to get and not the worm," replied Fatso.

"You a smart fellow," Bert replied.

Fatso said, "Okay, he's back there. I'll press the button to open his door for you, but first you have to tell me what did Tarzan say to Jane when he saw the elephants coming?"

"Here come the elephants," Bert replied. "That's an old one, Fatso. You need to get some new material." He walked to the back of the store and knocked on Trigger's door.

"Come on in," Trigger shouted. When he saw it was Sheriff Sterling he rose, shook hands, and said, "Good to see you Bert. How can I help you?"

The two sat and Bert said, "This thing with Mr. Lee is troubling me. I'm sure you heard the news releases yesterday. In addition to him driving that brown Chevy, there's now a helicopter in the picture. I don't know how it fits in, but I just feel something's up and I'm not sure what it is. Do you think of anything more you might be able to share that would help me?"

Trigger thought for a moment and then said, "Bert, I didn't say anything about it when we talked before, but when I first met Mr. Lee he stopped here at the store with a couple more men. They were driving a large semi truck. I have no idea what was in the truck, but I guess it could conceivably have been a small helicopter. That's purely a guess. I have no reason to know. And

I will go ahead now and tell you that he did indeed get a brown Chevy from me. I couldn't see any harm in providing him a car. Does that help?"

"It sure does," Bert said. "I'd almost bet that truck was hauling the helicopter. One of the guys at the Slusher farm described it as being a small one. I bet it's designed to be transported in a truck. You have no idea where they were headed?"

Trigger said, "Wish I could help you there, but I really have no idea whatsoever.'

Bert stood, shook hands with Trigger, and said, "You've been very helpful. I really thank you Trigger." He then left Trigger's office and started walking back through the grocery.

Fatso saw him and shouted, "Okay Bert, I got one more for you. Where do baby elephants come from?"

Bert thought but kept walking.

"Baby elephants come from big storks," shouted Fatso with a giggle.

Bert replied as he reached the door, "That's a little better, Fatso, you keep at it."

• • •

Maw Johnson was getting very nervous. It certainly wasn't like her two boys to stay out this long without her knowing. Sometimes they went on hunting trips and stayed several days camping out, but she always knew about those. This was really not like them at all. She was beginning to really worry that something bad had happened to them. She looked once again at her watch . . . it said 11 am. She'd give them one more hour and then call the sheriff.

• • •

11:30 am

Bert sat with Fred at Creech Cafe. The two were going to the ceremony together so Bert thought he'd have lunch with Fred before they left.

"You got the certificate all ready to go," the sheriff asked.

Fred replied, "Right here." He patted the attaché sitting in the chair beside them.

"You got any better feeling about the mysterious Mr. Lee," Fred asked.

"No," replied Bert. "I still think he's planning to

pull something at the ceremony, but I can't get any more information to locate him. Yeah, I'm worried."

The server brought two big plates with each having a club sandwich and french fried onion rings. She said, "Can I get you boys anything else? You want something cold to drink or are you okay with the coffee?"

Fred looked at Bert. Bert then said, "I'm okay with coffee . . . you Fred?"

Fred nodded. The two ate their lunch and continued with their chit-chat.

Bert looked at his watch and said, "Well, Fred, it's 12:15. By the time we get to the farm it'll be close to 1 o'clock. I wanted to be there no later than 1 just to make sure everything looks good and to talk with the FBI agents. Okay with you if we take off?"

At that moment Bert's cell phone rang.

"This is Sheriff Sterling," he said. He then listened for a couple of minutes and said, "Okay Rosie. Is Posey there yet?"

The sheriff nodded his head positively and said, "Here's what I want you to do. You and Preacher Puss leave immediately and go to the Johnson's farm. Old Maw Johnson sometimes gets things confused, and she's not the brightest person, so I really doubt that the information is accurate, but we can't take a chance. It's still almost 2 hours before the ceremony, so you should have plenty of time to drive to her house and talk with her and still get to the Slusher farm by no later than 1:30. If you do find out anything you think creditable please call me immediately and we'll act on it. I hate to ask you to do this at the last minute, but we really don't have any other available deputies. We've got em all stationed somewhere to cover security for the ceremony. But I think everything will be fine. Is that okay with you?"

Bert nodded again and disconnected the call. He then told Fred, "That was Rosie saying that old Maw Johnson over on the other side of Pine Mountain called to say her boys were missing and that they had a neighbor that had a helicopter and a brown Chevy. Now the part about her boys missing I can believe, but I would bet she just heard the media report about the helicopter and Chevy and just threw that in to get us over there. And, I guess it worked. Rosie's sister Posey was already in the office to cover for her while she took Preacher Puss to the ceremony, so I told Rosie to leave right now and check things out with Maw Johnson and then come on over to the Slusher Farm. If all goes well she should get there no later than about 1:30."

"Sounds good to me," Fred replied. He stood and picked up his attaché. The two friends left for the Slusher farm.

•••

I was really excited. My big day was here. I even cooperated when Rosie wanted to go ahead and put my uniform on before we left so that her sister Posey could see me in it.

Posey said, "Isn't she just a doll? That Mrs. Cavanaugh sure outdid herself on this one. I bet after the media get through taking pictures of Preacher Puss in that uniform Mrs. Cavanaugh will have more business than she can take care of sewing pet uniforms. Preacher Puss is just so adorable!"

Rosie replied, "She sure is. I've already taken about 25 pictures of her myself. Now Posey you take good care of everything. Preacher Puss and I should be back no later than 5 o'clock. I'll tell you all about it then." Rosie grabbed me up and we headed for her car. I felt like a million dollars!

Rosie had baked a big box of cookies to take to the ceremony. She placed the box in the passenger seat of her cruiser and I got to sit on top of it. I could see out! When we got on the four-lane Harlan by-pass we had to stop at a red light. A car pulled up beside us on my side. I looked over at it. There were two young girls in it, one driving and the other in the passenger seat. They both immediately started pointing at me and laughing. I was embarrassed. I stuck my tongue out at them, but they kept giggling. Rosie reached over, petted me, and said, "Now Preacher Puss, don't you pay attention to those girls. They just never saw a deputy sheriff like you before. They're laughing because you look so cute in your uniform."

That made me feel better, but I continued to give them a mean look while sticking my tongue out at them.

The light changed and we continued to the Johnson farm.

● ● ●

Billy Bob whispered to Bubba, "You sleep any last night?"

Bubba replied, "Not a wink. My hands done gone numb. Can't feel a thing, and I never could sleep while I's sitting."

"Same with me, Bubba. I shore am sore. You reckon we might get out of this alive?"

Bubba said, "Don't rightly know. Them Chin-e-men seem awful mean....with them guns and all. Just don't rightly know. You reckon Maw called the law by now?"

"Yeah, I feel sure she has. She'd know by now that something was wrong," said Billy Bob.

Bubba said, "Well, I shore wish they'd show up. I don't know how much longer we can hold out like this. I done peed my pants"

Billy Bob nodded in agreement.

• • •

It sure is a pretty ride over Pine Mountain. The trees and bushes are so beautiful. I'm thankful to get to ride with Rosie to the Johnson place. I am a bit worried about making it back on time to the Slusher farm, but I'm sure they won't start the ceremony without us.

After crossing Pine Mountain and driving another few miles Rosie came to the mailbox on the right side of the road that said Johnson on it. She pulled in the driveway and continued up the gravel road to the farm house. She parked in front and said to me, "Preacher

Puss, you stay here and guard the car. I won't be long."
She then got out, walked up on the porch, and knocked
on the door. It opened, and I saw a woman shake hands
with Rosie and then the two went inside and closed the
door.

"Deputy Cain, I'm just worried to death. My boys
never stay gone this long without telling me where
they're going. I just know something bad has happened
to them."

"Now, now Mrs. Johnson, don't you worry. We'll
find them. Just tell me what you know about the
helicopter and the brown Chevy."

Maw replied, "Well, I ain't seen the hell-e-copter,
but I shore have heard it. Old Mr. Stepp in the farm
next to ours rent out his farm for a couple of weeks.
When the renters arrived, Billy Bob and Bubba went
over and welcomed them....seemed like the thing to
do. When they got there they found out the men were
Chi-nee-men and they had one of them hell-e-copter
things. They told my boys that they used it to fly over
trees looking for timber. I guess they was gonna buy the
timber rights for their company. They even promised
to take the boys for a ride in it. We even had em over
for supper last Saturday. They seemed nice enough...
but did seem a little strange."

The color was draining from Rosie's face as she said, "When was the last time you saw your boys?"

"They took off yesterday afternoon after we heard the announcement on the radio about the FBI looking for a brown Chevy and hell-e-copter. We knew them Chi-nee-men drove a brown Chevy and that they had a hell-e-copter. But we didn't want to cause them any trouble if they was really what they said they were. So I told the boys to go snoop on em.....try and find out what they was really up to. Ain't heard a word from em since then. I'm worried to death."

The color continued to drain from Rosie's face....it was getting white as snow.

Maw said, "Deputy, you feel okay. You don't look so good."

"I'm fine," lied Rosie as she pulled her cell phone out. "I've got to call the Sheriff to report this."

"Hey Bert, Rosie here, I'm at the Johnson farm and have just talked with Mrs. Johnson. I think we've located Mr. Lee, the helicopter, and the brown Chevy. Everything Mrs. Johnson tells me makes perfect sense. She says her boys went to the Stepp farm yesterday afternoon to snoop on renters that recently moved in, and that those renters drove a brown Chevy and had a helicopter. They told the brothers that the chopper was for doing timber surveying. I know it's about 1 o'clock now and I don't have much time left to get to the ceremony, but I think while I'm here I should go to the Stepp farm and investigate what's going on. Do you think you could hold up the ceremony for a bit if I'm running late?"

Rosie nodded and then said, "Great, Bert, I'll call you as soon as I know anything." She ended the call and said to Maw, "Mrs. Johnson, I'm going over to the Stepp farm to check on things. Don't you worry, I'll give you a call soon as I learn anything. You've been a great help, and I feel certain your sons will be fine. Thanks again."

I saw Rosie open the door and come quickly out and get in the car. "Preacher Puss, we gotta make one more stop before going to your ceremony. I think we might have some bad guys at the Stepp farm, just a couple of miles from here. Bert told me that he and Fred were already at the Slusher farm and that he'd delay the start until we could get there. So don't you worry, you'll still get to have your big ceremony....it'll just be delayed a tad."

I was concerned. Rosie was going to check out some bad guys. That sounded to me like she could get hurt. That would be terrible.

Rosie and I got back on the main road and drove a short distance until we came to the mailbox that said Stepp. She started to pull into their driveway, but there was a brown Chevy parked in it. Rosie pulled her cruiser across the driveway in front of the Chevy. Our car was barely off the main road. Rosie said to me, "Now Deputy Puss, I want you to stay in the car. I'm going to walk up the driveway and see what's going on here. I'll be back shortly and we'll head to your ceremony." She gave me a nice pet, and I meowed approvingly and swished my tail. She got out of the car and started walking up the driveway. I was still very worried. I sure hope she'll be okay. I really love Rosie.

CHAPTER 21
HARLAN COUNTY, KENTUCKY

Wednesday Afternoon

Bert looked at his watch, which read 1:45. He had not heard from Rosie for the past 45 minutes. The mayor was standing by his side, and there were probably around 30 other people in the Slusher farm house great room. All those from the farm were here, except for Charlie still keeping guard on the gate, and all the media people. Bert said to Fred, "Mr. Mayor, I think I'll go ahead and announce that we're likely to be delayed a bit."

"Probably a good idea," Fred said.

Bert moved to the center of the room and then shouted with a loud voice, "Ladies and gentlemen, could I have your attention for a moment." The room grew quiet. "Our special guest, Preacher Puss, is riding here with my deputy Rosie Cain. They are on a call on the other side of Pine Mountain. I had a call from Rosie a few minutes ago saying they might be delayed a few minutes. I just wanted to keep you informed. We'll begin the ceremony just as soon as they arrive. It shouldn't be long. Thank you for your patience.

FBI agents Eaton and McKay walked over to Bert. Agent Eaton said, "I hope there's no trouble."

Bert replied, "Hi Clair, I hope not." He then filled the two of them in on what Rosie had told him from the Johnson farm. The two agents looked very concerned.

"If we don't hear something from her by 2 pm I think we should send a couple of cars over there to see what's going on," said Agent McKay.

Bert, Fred, and Agent Eaton all nodded in agreement.

• • •

Rosie finally reached the end of the Stepp's driveway and saw the home. She noticed that the barn, over to the right of the home, was all closed up. She walked up on the porch and knocked on the door.

An Asian fellow opened the door and said, "Yes, officer, how may I help you?"

Rosie replied, "I'm deputy sheriff Rosie Cain. I'm responding to a call from Mrs. Johnson, your neighbor. She says that her two sons left home yesterday afternoon coming to your farm to inquire about an announcement on the radio that the FBI were looking for a brown Chevy and a helicopter. She said that you had both. I noticed the brown Chevy parked at the end of your driveway."

"Please come in, Deputy Cain," Colonel Lee replied. "We can talk."

The two then stepped into the house.

Rosie was then immediately grabbed by Yie and Gim. Yie grabbed her left arm and Gim her right arm. They then jerked the handcuffs from her belt and cuffed her hands behind her back.

Rosie protested, "You're making a huge mistake! The sheriff knows where I am, and dozens of lawmen will be here in minutes."

Colonel Lee looked at his watch. It read 1:45. He said, "It's time for the mission. Bring the deputy with us to the barn. We'll secure her there and get underway."

There was a yell from the back bedroom "Help. Help. Please help us!"

The three Koreans ignored the yell and pushed Rosie in front of them and out the door. They walked to the barn, opened the doors, and positioned Rosie beside a water trough located at the side of the barn's front. There was a water line running to the trough. Colonel Lee asked Rosie, "Where is the key to your handcuffs?"

Rosie said, "In my shirt pocket."

Lee reached in the pocket and extracted the key. He unlocked the cuff on her right hand,, placed it around the water line, and locked it there. He then stuck the key in his pants pocket. He then pushed Rosie down into a sitting position beside the trough and said, "That'll hold you while we complete our mission. After we get back and leave the farm you and the Johnson boys will be found....but we'll be long gone." He grinned at her, turned, and yelled at Colonel Gim, "Get the helicopter out of the barn. Yie and I will load the bombs and then be off. You watch the deputy and monitor the radio. We should be back in less than a half hour."

Gim nodded in agreement and started walking to the fork lift.

● ● ●

I was really worried now. Rosie had been gone longer than necessary. I just strongly felt that bad guys had her at the Stepp house. But I couldn't get out of the car . . . what was I going to do?

Just then the mailman drove up. Rosie's cruiser was blocking his way to the mailbox. I watched as he parked his car behind ours and got out with mail in his hand. He walked on the driver's side of our car and then over to the mailbox and placed the mail in it. As he turned to walk back to his car he looked in the cruiser and saw me sitting on the cookie box in the passenger seat. He got a big grin on his face and walked around to the passenger door. He looked in the window and said, "Now aren't you the fancy cat. First one I ever saw in a police uniform."

I started pawing on the window and meowing real loud. The mailman got a concerned look on his face and said, "Kitty, are you okay?"

I pawed quicker and meowed louder.

He reached down, placed his hand on the door handle, and slowly opened the door. It was all the chance I needed. I jumped quickly through the crack in the door, under the mailman's arm, and hit the ground running. He said, "Hey kitty, you get back here."

I ran as fast as my four legs would carry me. Soon I got to the end of the driveway and saw the house. I looked over to the right of the house and saw the barn. The barn doors were open and a forklift was just sitting down a pallet with a helicopter on it. And then I saw Rosie. She was sitting on the ground beside a water trough. I could tell one of her arms was behind her, and I guessed they had her tied to something. She didn't see me.

I slowly crept up to the side of the barn front. Rosie was tied up on the other side. I peeked around the front corner of the barn and saw her. She was watching as two men were picking up something in the barn. A third man was moving the forklift to park it on the other side. I looked up at the helicopter. It was still on the wooden pallet. It's doors were open. I knew I couldn't untie Rosie, so I thought the best thing I could do would be to attempt to cause these bad men trouble. If I did that, maybe they wouldn't be able to harm her. So I made my move. I quickly ran up to the passenger side of the helicopter and leaped up through the open door. I was really scared, and had no idea what I might be able to do, but thought that being here in the helicopter might provide me an opportunity. I jumped to the very back of the cockpit. There was a small compartment there and I fit in it perfectly. I pulled my tail down between my legs, and stuck my head up enough to get my eyes above the compartment wall so I could see the cockpit, and waited.

Colonel Yie yelled, "Hey Gim, give us a hand mounting these bombs. We really need to be careful. One good jolt and we'll all be history."

Gim came running around to the front of the right skid. Yie was carrying one of the bombs toward it. When he got there Gim grabbed the loop at the end of the rope that held the bomb and placed it over the end of the skid. Yie then gently placed the bomb on the pallet and curled the rope on top of it. Gim then moved quickly to the front of the left skid and assisted Lee as he positioned the second bomb.

Colonel Lee then said, "Okay, I've got 2 pm. I think we're ready to go. Yie, do you have the remote control?"

Yie grabbed the remote from his vest pocket, held it out and said, "Right here. We're good to go."

Colonel Gim, standing in front of the helicopter, held up his hand held radio and said, "Let me know if you need me to do anything."

"Will do," Colonel Lee shouted as he and Colonel Yie jumped into the cockpit.

I was terrified. And then it got worse. The man sitting in the left seat reached down and pushed a lever and there was a loud noise and everything started to vibrate. The man in the right seat gave a thumbs-up signal to the man on the ground, and then we began rising slowly into the air. I was very thankful I went to the bathroom right before we left home, otherwise I'm sure the compartment I was in would have gotten real nasty. Apparently the two men could talk to each other using some kind of intercom, but having extremely keen hearing I could just make out what they said. The one on the left said, "Okay, Yie, are the ropes to the bombs unraveling okay?" The man on the right then looked through the open door beside him and replied, "Perfectly. Both bombs are now hanging at the end of their ropes. When I press this big red button on the remote they'll be released by the actuators in the center of the ropes. Everything looks good. Take her on up."

Colonel Lee responded, "Will do. I'm going to fly low to the target. I'll keep her at about 500 feet. No one should be able to spot us. When we get to the Slusher house, I'll take her up high so we can release the bombs without being impacted by the explosions."

"Roger that," replied Yie

My eyes were big as saucers. How thankful I was that neither man looked back and noticed me. And if they spotted me now I'm sure they'd just toss me out of this thing. I'd be one dead cat! What was I going to do?

I thought about what they said. Apparently they were headed for the Slusher house, and planned to bomb it. All my friends and all the cats there would be killed. I sure couldn't let that happen. But how could I stop it?

I remembered the one guy on the right say that when he pressed the big red button the bombs would drop. It was then that I knew what I had to do.

• • •

The Mayor walked up to Bert and said, "Sheriff, I've got a few minutes past 2 pm. And we've still not heard a word from Rosie. What are your thoughts?"

Bert replied, "I called a moment ago and talked with Mrs. Johnson. She said she had not heard anything further since Rosie left her place. I think I'll call for a couple of our deputies to leave their security posts and drive to the Stepp farm and see what's going on."

"I think that would be in order," Fred said. "What are we going to do about the ceremony?"

"I think we just hang on for a while. We'll know something for sure after the deputies check out things. If Rosie and Preacher Puss don't show by 3 we'll just have to postpone the ceremony. I'd sure hate that, but I don't know what else to do."

Agent Eaton walked over to Fred and Bert and said, "We're monitoring the video from the drone and haven't spotted anything that looks at all suspicious. Anything further we could be doing?"

Bert thought a moment and said, "No, not that I can think of. Just keep watching."

• • •

"I think we should be approaching the clearing for the farm house," Colonel Lee said as he looked at his GPS.

"Yeah, the timing is about right," replied Colonel Yie as he extracted the remote control from his vest pocket. He held it out in his left hand.....getting ready to press the red button with his right hand forefinger.

I looked and saw the remote control held out in the left hand of the guy on my right. It was being held about midway between the two men....perfect for me! It was just about time for me to act.

It was then that I heard the guy on the left say, "Okay, Yie, we're right at the clearing. I'll start taking us up to a suitably high altitude to drop the bombs."

This was it. It was now or never. I quickly positioned myself on the top of the compartment box, and then with a mighty leap pushed as hard as I could with my back feet directly toward the remote control. My right paw was extended and landed directly on the red button. I felt the front of the helicopter immediately rock upward as the bombs were released. The man holding the remote slapped my head with his right hand....and it hurt bad. The man on the left released the controls and grabbed at me with both hands.

And then the bombs exploded! Since we were still at only 500 feet altitude we felt it immediately. The shock wave violently shook us. The helicopter started to roll, and to drop toward the ground. The man on the left released me and grabbed the controls again and worked frantically to gain control of the falling chopper. We were just about to crash into the ground when control returned. At the time, the craft was turned on its right side. I saw the ground coming at us quickly, and made the decision to jump out the open door.

•••

Agent Eaton came running up to Bert and said, "Our drone has just spotted a helicopter headed our way." The agent had a headset on listening to the drone operator report what he saw.

She continued, "Hold on, the chopper is now right at the end of the tree line and something just dropped from it."

There was then a deafening noise and the entire house shook like an earthquake had hit it.

"What the Sam Hill was that?" Bert asked. Everyone in the room covered their heads thinking the roof might fall.

Clair Eaton said, "The drone operator said it looked like two objects fell from the helicopter and exploded right on the fence line. He said there were huge craters where they fell. He now says the helicopter lost control from the explosions and started to fall and crash, but at the last second recovered and was now flying away. He said something else.....he thought he saw an object fall from it just as it recovered. He's taking the drone over to the area now to see what he can pick up."

Agent McKay came running into the great room with a portable monitor that was picking up the video signal from the drone. Everyone in the room tried to gather around her to see the screen. The camera on the drone was pointed toward the ground as it rushed over to the area where the bombs were dropped. Suddenly there appeared on the monitor some kind of small creature moving slowly on the ground. The drone operator zoomed the camera in to capture the animal. Preacher Puss filled the screen, looking directly up toward the drone!

Bert shouted, "Ladies and Gentlemen, may I present Harlan County Deputy Sheriff Preacher Puss! I don't know what she did or how she did it, but I feel certain that cat just saved the lives of everyone in this room!"

Fred started clapping. Everyone else quickly joined in. There were shouts of praise, and laughter broke out everywhere.

Bert ran to the back door to go out and bring the hero in.

Barbara Clark, news anchor for the Lexington television station WKYT, shouted, "That's the cutest deputy sheriff I ever saw. Look at that uniform. And a hero too! What a story....I can't wait to get pictures and an interview with her."

• • •

Colonel Gim got a call from Colonel Lee, who said, "Gim, we've encountered a problem. Go immediately and get the car and bring it up to the barn. I just started heading back, as soon as we get there we need to leave. The authorities are on the way. Do you copy?"

Gim replied, "Copy Lee, I'll have the car here waiting."

He then shouted to Rosie, "You're not going any place. I'll be right back." He then took off running down the driveway.

Rosie always prided herself in being prepared. She always wore a leg pocket that held two things. One was a can of mace, the other was an extra handcuff key. When Gim was out of sight she reached down with her free right hand and pulled up her right pants leg. She then reached into the pocket that was strapped on her leg above her shoe and extracted the key to the handcuffs. They were soon off, and she then pulled out the mace. The Koreans had taken her gun, but failed to frisk her. Lucky for her! She then got back down in position where she had been, sitting beside the water trough with her left hand behind her. She was holding the can of mace in that hand.

The brown Chevy came speeding up the driveway and over beside the barn. Gim got out, walked over beside Rosie and said, "Good, you're still here. We'll soon be gone." At that moment Gim heard a 'wop, wop, wop' and looked up trying to spot the helicopter.

Rosie quickly pulled the can of mace out and sprayed it directly into his face. He fell to the ground screaming in agony. Rosie took off running as fast as she could for her cruiser. She arrived at it and jumped in, started up the motor, and sped off. It was only then that she noticed that Preacher Puss was not in the car. When she first got in she figured she was sleeping in the back seat, but now realized she wasn't in the car. She pulled out her cell phone and called the sheriff.

"Hey Bert, I just got free from being held captive. I'm back in my cruiser headed your way. But I got a big problem . . . Preacher Puss is not with me!."

Rosie listened a moment, got a huge grin, and said, "So the ole girl struck again. Unbelievable! I can't wait to hear the story. But you need to know that I just maced one of the bad guys. When I left he was waiting for the helicopter to get back, and then they were all going to make a run for it in that brown Chevy. He was lying on the ground in agony from the mace. Also, Mrs. Johnson's two sons are held captive in one of the Stepp farm house bedrooms."

Rosie listened again to Bert and then said, "Good, I think I can hear their sirens now. Please call them and relay what's happened. They should be able to grab all three crooks and release the Johnson boys."

In about another minute the two sheriff's cars sped by Rosie headed to the Stepp farm. They each waved as they passed her.

Rosie thought, *how fortunate we've been. The attack was somehow stopped by Preacher Puss. The bad guys will be caught, and the Johnson boys found and released. And we're still on for the ceremony to honor Preacher Puss, who now is more than ever a true hero. I can't wait to get there.* She sped up.

• • •

Deputy Sheriff Kyle Potter was driving one of the cruisers responding to Sheriff Sterling's call to go to the Stepp farm. The other cruiser was driven by Deputy Sheriff Mousy Giles. Just as the two cars arrived at the driveway leading to the Stepp farm house they saw headlights coming down the driveway toward them. Kyle was the lead car and pulled into the driveway far enough to allow Mousy to pull in behind him. The moment the cars stopped the two deputies jumped out of their cars. Both cars had their lights flashing and headlights still on. Kyle stood at the front, left side of his cruiser while Mousy had run to the right front side.

They each stood with guns drawn and pointed straight toward the oncoming headlights.

Colonel Lee, driving the brown Chevy, said, "I think we have a decision to make. We can either try shooting it out with these guys, or we can turn ourselves over to them." All three Koreans had handguns drawn. Their car had almost reached the deputies.

Colonel Gim spoke, "I'll go along with what you think, but I believe in a shootout we'd likely not come out the winner. Even if we did, and made it back home my guess would be that our Supreme Leader would have us executed for failing our mission. Frankly, I think we'd be better off in jail here. That's just my opinion."

Lee and Yie nodded in approval. Colonel Yie said, "I agree. We made our best effort, but failed. Lets just end it now and pay the consequences."

Colonel Lee stopped the car. Each Korean rolled down his window and tossed his gun out.

Kyle then shouted, "Get out of the car with your hands in the air . . . Do it now!"

The car doors opened and all three Koreans got out with hands up.

Mousy walked over to them while Kyle kept his gun pointed. Mousy handcuffed each Korean and then took them to his cruiser and placed them in the back seat.

Kyle spoke to Mousy, "You take em to Jail....I'll go up to the house and get the Johnson brothers."

"Will do," Mousy replied, and then got in his cruiser, backed out, and sped off toward Harlan.

Kyle first backed the brown Chevy back up the driveway, and then drove his cruiser to the house, parked, and ran to the door. As he entered the house he heard shouting, "Help. Help. Please help us." He walked to the bedroom and found the brothers tied to the bedposts and sitting on the floor.

"You guys ready to go?" Kyle asked as he started untying them.

"We shore is, Kyle. You be a sight for sore eyes," Billy Bob said.

"We so sore and numb I doubt we can stand," Bubba said.

Kyle replied, "Take your time. Just sit there a moment and move around a bit to get the blood circulating again. You'll be okay."

After about ten minutes of continued sitting while telling Kyle what had happened to them the brothers stood up, and the three left the house, got in the cruiser, and headed to see Maw.

Maw ran to the door when she heard the knock. She had been listening to the radio hoping to learn something new regarding her boys. When she opened the door she first saw Deputy Potter who said, "Mrs. Johnson, I've got a couple of deliveries to make to you." He then stood aside and let the brothers hug their mother.

"My word," Maw said after big hugs and kisses from each boy, "I was beginning to think I might not see you again. Praise the Lord! And Kyle Potter I sure thank you for bringing them back to me. I'll never forget it. Now you boys get in there and take a bath.... you stink!"

"Just doing my duty, Mrs. Johnson. You enjoy them . . . and you all be safe," Kyle said as he turned to go to his cruiser.

CHAPTER 22
HARLAN COUNTY, KENTUCKY

Wednesday Afternoon

Rosie pulled up to the guard gate at the Slusher farm. "Hey Charlie, I'm running a tad late."

From his window in the guard house Charlie replied, "You sure are. You just missed the big explosion. It shook my little house here so bad I thought it was going to collapse. Gunsmoke called me and said not to worry, that there had been an explosion over on the Southwest boundary but no one was hurt. I'm not sure what it was all about."

"I think I know," Rosie replied. "We'll fill you in later. I need to get to the ceremony....I think they're holding it up for me."

"Sure, you go right on in. I'll phone Gunsmoke and tell him you're on the way," Charlie said as he pushed the button to raise the gate.

•••

"Okay, I'll tell everybody. Thanks Charlie," Gunsmoke said. He then turned to Bert and said, "Charlie said Rosie just cleared the gate."

Bert looked at his watch, which read 2:45 pm, and said loudly, "Folks, Rosie will be here in a couple of minutes, and we'll get the show on the road."

All those assembled nodded their heads, some cheered, some clapped. I sat proudly in the center of the room on a table that had been placed there for me. About 15 of my cat friends were playing around the table. The media had their cameras and microphones all arranged on tripods in front of me. There was a podium beside me, and Mayor Knapp was approaching it carrying my framed certificate.

Rosie came running into the room and shouted, "Really sorry I'm late, but super glad to be here!" Everyone cheered as she ran up to me and gave me a real big hug. She then started petting me and said, "Preacher Puss, you are one amazing cat. I have no idea how you did it, but you certainly managed to save the day. I know everyone in this house would be dead right now if you had not somehow intervened. I sure hope someday we'll learn how you did it. You are a super hero." And then she leaned down and gave me a big kiss . . . right on my head! I know I blushed, but fortunately no one could tell.

The cameras were rolling, capturing Rosie's reunion with me. I was sure proud. I bet we'll be on television and in the newspapers! I'll be famous!

Rosie continued to stand beside me as Mayor Knapp cleared his throat loudly and then said, "Ladies and Gentlemen, we are gathered here today to honor a very, very special member of the Harlan County Sheriff's Department. When we planned this ceremony we had no idea that Preacher Puss would demonstrate so dramatically her ability to subdue crooks and save lives. But that she just did. I've been told that three foreign nationals have been taken to the Harlan County jail after Preacher Puss intervened to stop their attempt to bomb this house. The earthquake-like jar you felt and explosion you heard just moments ago were two bombs that dropped on the fence line....but were intended to drop right on top this house. Somehow, this specially talented cat caused the premature release of those bombs, and thus saved us from sure destruction."

Mayor Knapp then lifted the framed certificate and said, "Preacher Puss, this piece of paper just doesn't come anywhere close to rewarding you enough. But

I know I speak for everyone in this room when I say we're truly grateful for all you've done in the past, and especially for what you did today. You are a cat with talents beyond our understanding. All we can say is 'Thank You'. I will now read the certificate:

Because of her demonstrated ability to subdue crooks and for her devoted duty,
The feline member of the Harlan County Sheriff's Department named
PREACHER PUSS
is hereby granted the title of Honorary Harlan County Deputy Sheriff

and it is signed by Harlan County Sheriff J. Bert Sterling and myself as Mayor of Harlan."

There was tremendous applause. It kinda scared me, but I knew everyone meant well. I looked over at Rosie and meowed loudly my approval. The mayor sat the framed certificate beside me on the table, and lots of pictures were taken. I was not even self-conscious any more about my uniform. What a great day . . . one I'll never forget!

And then Barbara Clark, news anchor for Lexington television station WKYT, came up with a microphone in her hand and a guy holding a television camera behind her. She placed the microphone between herself and Rosie and said, "Deputy Cain, this represents quite a unique honor for Preacher Puss. It isn't every day that a cat is made an honorary deputy sheriff. I have two questions for you. First, how did she get the unusual name? And second, could you tell us about what happened today with the attempted bombing?"

Rosie then answered both questions for Ms. Clark. I purred my approval, and I'm pretty sure the camera got me! I'll be on TV! I hope Bandit and Sylvester see me!

CHAPTER 23
HARLAN, KENTUCKY

Wednesday, one week later

Sheriff Sterling had called a meeting in his office. In addition to the sheriff, Mayor Fred Knapp, Deputy Kyle Potter, FBI agent Clair Eaton, Gunsmoke and Booger Slusher, a reporter named Sam Asher from the **Harlan Daily Enterprise**, and Rosie and I were all gathered around the front of Bert's desk. Rosie held me in her lap, giving me loving strokes. I purred my approval loudly.

The sheriff began, "Friends, I thank each of you for being here. I know you are all very busy people, so I'll try and make our meeting short. I called the meeting because I felt the need to go over the events of last Wednesday. As each of you are well aware, we came very, very close to a major tragedy . . . over 30 people could well have been killed. And we have our friend Deputy Preacher Puss here to thank for saving us."

Everyone in the room looked at me. I was embarrassed, but pleased and proud. I swished my tail and uttered a nice meow in approval. Rosie continued to pet me.

Bert continued, "Because of the seriousness of the event, I thought we should get together just to review what happened and to try and discover if we're missing doing anything. I would appreciate any comments from any of you. If our office phone rings or if anyone comes into the office we'll have to excuse Rosie to step out and cover it, we couldn't schedule Posey to be here this morning to cover for her."

Everyone looked at Rosie, smiled, and nodded in approval. I hoped I wouldn't lose my lap!

The sheriff said, "First, I want to thank all the media for covering the event so well. And Sam, I hope you will be sure to acknowledge our thanks in the article you'll produce about today's meeting."

Sam Asher said, "Sure will Bert. Believe me, it was a pleasure. I know our article in the *Enterprise* was read by a record number of people."

"I'm sure it was," Bert replied, "and our office and that of Mayor Knapp have been swamped with letters and phone calls from all the coverage we received nationwide. It was indeed excellent press for our town and county." Bert looked at Fred.

Fred said, "Was it ever! It far, far exceeded my expectations."

Rosie spoke up, "I might just add that as a result of all the publicity Mrs. Cavanaugh now has tons of orders for pet uniforms. I talked with her recently and she told me that she had contracted with two other ladies to sew for her just to help keep up with the orders. She also mentioned to me that her cat, Sylvester, now banned from coming into her home was watching her TV while perched outside on a ledge at the bottom of the living room window and saw Preacher Puss in her uniform at the ceremony. Mrs. Cavanaugh said Sylvester immediately jumped down from the window and stayed gone two days. I guess seeing Preacher Puss on TV was just too much for him. Also, my mother and her pet raccoon in Tennessee saw the ceremony coverage on the Knoxville television station."

I thought, *Thank you Lord, they saw me!*

Bert then said, "Also, Agent Eaton told me that the government got information from North Korea that Kim Jong-un executed the commander of his air force, General Ri Pyong-rok. So I guess ole 'Rocket Man' was terribly upset over yet another failed mission.

The sheriff continued, "One thing the public is not aware of right now are the developments that have occurred with the three North Korean colonels. Just so we have everything about them in proper perspective I'd like to ask Deputy Kyle Potter to first review what happened when they were arrested last Wednesday."

Kyle replied, "Well, Mousy Giles and I arrived at the Stepp Farm and had just entered their driveway when we encountered the Koreans coming down the narrow, one-lane driveway attempting to escape. When they approached us they stopped their car, threw out their weapons, and surrendered without incident. They were very cooperative, and continued to be so until Mousy got them back to the jail."

"Thanks Kyle," Bert said. "I spent a good deal of time talking with them and discovered that they were very much like the seven other ex-North Korean soldiers now employed at the Slusher Farm, having been granted political asylum by our government. The nutcase leader of North Korea, Kim Jong-un, was still really highly disturbed by the seven failing in their missions for him and now living good and productive lives. He still wanted revenge, and conjured up a scheme whereby these three colonels in his air force would come here and fly a helicopter to the Slusher farm and bomb it when all the deserters, as he called them, were present. He didn't care how many others he killed in so doing.

And it almost worked, but we'll get to that later. Right now I'd like to ask Special Agent Clair Eaton to explain what has happened to the colonels and their present status."

Agent Eaton started, "Thanks sheriff. Bert called me after his discussions with the Koreans. He told me that they were simply following orders from their madman leader, and that they were, in his opinion, basically good people and asked if I thought there would be a possibility of getting them granted political asylum. After thinking about the situation for a bit, I told him I thought that might be possible if they had productive employment and would not be a ward of the state."

"I knew the process for getting the political asylum granted," Bert said, "having gone through it with the other North Koreans. So I first had a meeting with Judge Oakes, and told him what we had in mind, and asked if he would consider dropping the criminal charges against the three contingent upon their being granted political asylum. He considered my request, and then got back to me that he would, also contingent upon their having productive employment. It was at that time that I made a phone call to the Slusher brothers." He then looked toward them.

Gunsmoke said, "Booger and I have had a truly great experience with all seven of the North Koreans we now have working for us at the farm. They are great people, and work very hard and earn their keep. We saw no reason why these three would be any different, and we certainly have work for them. Their lodging might be a little cramped for a while, but we'll construct a new building to house them, and it should be ready in about six months. We've talked with them, and have given our approval to start their employment immediately."

Bert replied, "Thanks guys. You are the greatest. As you all know, the process for political asylum takes a while, but everyone feels certain it will be granted. So, I'm really pleased and excited to announce today that the three North Korean colonels have been moved from our jail and are now in residence at the Slusher Farm, pending approval for political asylum."

All in the room clapped to express their approval.

"So having talked with them so much, and with their cooperation, I've also learned the real story of how Preacher Puss managed to stop their intended bombing of the Slusher farm house. And is it ever a story!"

I put on my proudest look! I really didn't know if anyone would ever know exactly what I did. I was excited . . . my story was going to be known!

Bert went on to tell the soldiers' version of what had happened, starting with Preacher Puss apparently jumping into the helicopter just before they took off on their mission, and then hiding in the small compartment in the back of the cockpit until it was almost time to drop the bombs. They said that just as they approached the fence line around the Slusher property they both saw a grey flash flying between them. They described how Yie was holding the bomb release remote control in his left hand and the cat managed to press the red button and released the bombs prematurely. They then explained that the helicopter almost crashed from the impact of the bombs exploding, and that just when they regained control and were just feet above the ground Preacher Puss jumped out.

"What an incredible story," said Mayor Knapp. But one thing I still don't understand, how did Preacher Puss get out of Rosie's cruiser? She does a lot of impossible things, but I don't think she can open car doors!"

Rosie spoke, "That's true, Fred. But just yesterday I learned how she did it. I was getting ready to take my cruiser to the car wash and was cleaning out all the papers and junk in it. I discovered a note that had fallen to the floor. The note was written by a mailman and it said he was sorry that he had opened my car door and let my cat out. He said he saw her sitting in the cruiser as he was delivering mail, and that she was pawing at the window and meowing loudly. He said he was just going to try and calm and pet her, but when he cracked the door she leaped out and ran up the driveway. He said he hoped I got her back safely and left his name and phone number. I did call him and thanked him, and assured him that Preacher Puss was safe."

"Absolutely remarkable," said Sam Asher. "What a story this will make."

"Another point I wanted to cover concerns old Mr. Stepp," Bert said. "Obviously he was contacted by someone in order to rent out his farm. We need to try and find out who that person or persons were. They certainly were working for Kim Jong-un, and we need to find and prosecute them. Agent Eaton will be following up on this."

Agent Eaton said, "Yes, and that information is off the record. Please don't disclose that in any news article." She looked toward Sam Asher. He nodded in agreement.

Agent Eaton continued, "One other thing I might add is that the government is going to give Bennie Sekao a reward of $2500 for providing the information about Colonel Lee. Mr. Sekao seemed totally shocked when I informed him."

Deputy Kyle Potter chuckled and said, "It's not every day he sees that kind of money. But he deserved it."

"A question I had was how the Johnson boys are doing," Fred asked.

Bert replied, "I called Maw Johnson a couple of days ago to ask. She said they had fully recovered from their experience, but were staying pretty close to home. But she did say they were really sorry they wouldn't be getting their ride in the helicopter."

Everyone chuckled, and then Sam Asher asked, "That brings up an interesting question. What will happen to the helicopter?"

Bert said, "Good question. We ran down the registration on the semi truck. The helicopter didn't have any numbers on it. The truck was registered to a company in Knoxville that does equipment sales and leasing. I talked with their manager and he checked the records and told me that the chopper and truck were bought from them. He said he remembered it as a very unusual transaction because the client paid cash and simply drove off with the chopper in the truck. I then checked with Tennessee to see if the truck registration had been transferred, and it had not. I did get a description of the guy that bought them, but it's pretty vanilla. I doubt we'll be able to track him down. So anyway, the way it stands now Harlan County owns the helicopter and truck. We've got them both at the Slusher farm. Since the three colonels are likely the only helicopter pilots in the county, I asked them if they would be willing to fly it on any police business we might have, and they agreed. We'll just keep the truck there in case we need to move the helicopter or have other need of it. So it looks like the Johnson boys might still get their helicopter rides."

"Let me know if they do," said Sam Asher, "i'd like to cover that."

"Certainly," Bert replied. "Anyone think of anything else?"

All nodded negatively and then the sheriff said, "Well, again, I really appreciate your being here....and thanks so much for all your cooperation. I'll keep you posted on any developments."

Everyone except Rosie stood, chatted a bit, and then started to move toward the door. Each person stopped where Rosie sat with me in her lap and gave me a nice pet and a word of appreciation. It was real nice. I am a blessed cat!

As Mayor Knapp gave me his pet he looked at Rosie and said, "You know what I think? I think someone should write a book about this astounding cat, and a good title for it would be *The Adventures of Preacher Puss.*"

CPSIA information can be obtained
at www.ICGtesting.com
Printed in the USA
FFOW01n0239050418
46126906-47195FF

9 780692 052549